"*You could have written.*"

"What was there to say? You left *me*, remember?"

"How could I forget?"

His casual tone infuriated Lindsey, and despite longing to know, she would die before giving him the satisfaction of knowing she cared enough to ask. It's nothing other than desire, she told herself. It has nothing to do with love.

ROBERTA LEIGH started writing when she was fourteen and has produced since then a great number of romantic novels, children's books and has won awards for her many television scripts. For many people that would be enough, but Roberta has also found time to paint, study graphology and be a mother to a now grown-up son.

She believes in writing about romance because "if one can put love into any book it will find an echo within the reader."

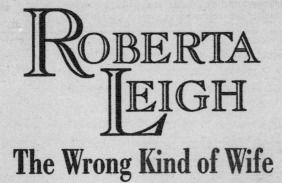

Roberta Leigh

The Wrong Kind of Wife

Harlequin Books

TORONTO • NEW YORK • LONDON
AMSTERDAM • PARIS • SYDNEY • HAMBURG
STOCKHOLM • ATHENS • TOKYO • MILAN
MADRID • WARSAW • BUDAPEST • AUCKLAND

ISBN 0-373-11725-6

THE WRONG KIND OF WIFE

Copyright © 1994 by Roberta Leigh.

First North American Publication 1995.

This edition published by arrangement with Harlequin Enterprises B.V.

® and TM are trademarks of the publisher. Trademarks indicated with ® are registered in the United States Patent and Trademark Office, the Canadian Trade Marks Office and in other countries.

Printed in U.S.A.

CHAPTER ONE

As LINDSEY handed over her charge card at the supermarket checkout, her thoughts were not centred on the bill but on how she was going to tell her husband she had to go to Paris again. It was the second time this month, and Tim had barely got over his annoyance at her last trip.

It wasn't as if she enjoyed going, but travelling to interview celebrities was part of her job as a television researcher, and if she wished to further her career there was no way she could refuse. Because of this she had just splashed out on an expensive bottle of wine, instead of the usual plonk, to accompany tonight's meal. Tim would appreciate it, and hopefully would be in a better humour when she broke the news.

Balancing the carrier bags in one hand, she unlocked the front door with the other. A smell of burning fat greeted her and she sighed. Tim was cooking again!

Hurrying into a kitchen so tiny one couldn't swing a cat in it, she saw him in the act of pouring a soggy black mess down the drain.

'Hello, sweetheart,' he greeted her, one hand raking back the errant lock of blond hair that was always falling across his forehead. 'I thought I'd make the supper for a change, but I guess I misread the recipe!'

'I wish you'd leave the cooking to me,' Lindsey retorted. She was tired, cold and hungry, and her temper was at flash-point. With an effort she controlled it and moved towards the sink. 'Fix me a drink, darling, and I'll clean up,' she said more gently.

'Let's have dinner out,' Tim said, putting his arms around her.

As always, his touch excited her, even though she found his suggestion irritating. Had he forgotten they were supposed to be economising?

'I've bought a stack of food,' she pointed out.

'It won't go to waste. Come on, sweetheart, it will do you good to relax.'

'I can relax better here. I've been out with a questionnaire the whole day.'

Tim frowned. 'I hate the thought of you tramping round the freezing streets while I sit in a warm office doing nothing.'

'Don't be silly. I'm only "tramping the streets" until I've finished my survey. And you don't do nothing all day—you work damned hard.'

'As dogsbody to a drunk! Beats me why Turlow hasn't been fired.'

'He's considered an institution,' Lindsey said drily. 'Though I heard a whisper that he'll be through in a year. And if you play your cards carefully——'

'I still won't get his job. I haven't enough experience to be political correspondent on a national daily.'

'Turlow wouldn't have chosen you as his assistant if he didn't think you capable of taking over from him. What's happened to your confidence? If you——'

Tim's mouth on hers silenced her, and though she was still cold and tired she responded to his touch.

'How hungry *are* you?' He nuzzled his face in her neck and breathed in the scent of her.

'For food, or——?'

'For or.'

'Getting hungrier by the second,' she murmured, relaxing as he swung her into his arms and carried her into the bedroom, the one place where they were assured of perfect harmony.

Their coming together was quick and intense, expressing the fierce need they still aroused in each other, and with Tim's manhood inside her Lindsey revelled in being the woman he loved, marvelling, as she so often did, that she was the one he had chosen to make his wife.

'I love you,' she whispered, running the tips of her fingers down his sweat-slicked skin. His sharp intake of breath and the swell of him inside her excited her, and she pressed her lips to the golden whorls of hair on his chest that arrowed down to his stomach.

Triggered by her touch, his thrusting movements grew stronger and he was no longer able to hold back, his body responding in a flash-flood of urgency that matched hers, sending them both spiralling among the stars, from which they seemed to descend a long time later.

Lindsey awoke first. Tim was lying on his side, an arm flung across her, his hand resting on her breast. Asleep, he looked younger than his twenty-six years. He often acted younger too, she reflected, then pushed aside the thought, feeling guilty for thinking it. Yet it was true. In every respect except years she was the more mature. Not surprising, given that she had spent most of her adolescence in an orphanage after her mother and step-father had been killed in a motorway crash. It had been a tough grounding, and it had required determination and tenacity to escape from it and win a scholarship to university.

Even now she cringed at the memory of the raw, naïve young girl she had been. Luckily her outward appearance had not given her away. Tall and fashionably thin, with wild, dark red hair cascading past her shoulders, blazing green eyes and a naturally voluptuous red mouth that drew attention to her pale, creamy skin, she had looked every inch the confident feminist of the eighties.

Her aura of self-assurance had deceived Tim as well, and after their marriage she had made an effort to put the bitter memories of the past behind her, determined not to let them sour the happy present; and though there were occasional times when they returned to haunt her, she allowed no one to be party to her tears.

As if sensing her thoughts, Tim stirred in his sleep and pulled her close, and with a returning surge of tenderness Lindsey snuggled into the warmth of him and switched her mind back to how they had met.

It had been at a party in Cambridge—where else would two people of disparate backgrounds cross paths? Tim had grown up on the family estate in Somerset, near the town of Evebury where his father owned a successful engineering plant.

Within moments of seeing Lindsey across the room, Tim had pushed his way across to her. She had been flattered that the best-looking man in the room had eyes only for her, and felt as if she were Delilah and Jezebel rolled into one!

An hour later they were seated in a small but expensive restaurant on the outskirts of town—one that was way out of the price-range of herself and her friends—and Tim had teased her for weeks afterwards about her appearing more interested in the menu than him!

It was untrue, of course. Her concentration on the food had been a device to hide her discomfiture, for it was the first time she had been taken anywhere so elegant, and by someone who was clearly at home there. She had always dated men from her own background and avoided mixing with the rich set.

But with Tim it had been different. He had disarmed her with his warmth and natural charm, his innate good manners that made him treat her as if she were someone special. And to him she *was* special, her sharp tongue and fiery spirit a great contrast to the girls he usually escorted. Within days they were in love, spending every possible moment together, and regarding their hours apart as wasted ones.

'You're so caring about everything,' he had commented on one occasion. 'When I'm with you I see the world through your eyes.'

'It isn't such a comfortable world as yours,' she had stated.

'I know, and I'm sad for you. I want you to be happy always, Lindsey.'

Lindsey had wanted this too, but was afraid it was not to be, for she knew her happiness was with Tim and did not believe their relationship would turn into a permanent commitment. She had grown up in too tough a school to believe in fairy-tales, and Cinderella was strictly a story in a book. So she was dumbfounded when he'd asked her to marry him.

She had accepted instantly, and they were married shortly after they graduated, with a small reception given by Tim's parents for their close family and a select few of their friends.

'A big wedding wouldn't be quite the thing,' Mrs Ramsden had explained with a cool smile. 'I mean, it isn't as if you have any family to invite...'

The implication being that, even if she had, they would have felt out of place and been unacceptable. Mrs Ramsden had not expressed her antipathy to Lindsey in any concrete manner, but Lindsey had sensed it the instant they met. Mr Ramsden had tried to be friendly, but since his wife was the dominant personality she realised she would never have anything other than a constrained relationship with either of them.

To begin with the knowledge had distressed her, making her nervous of saying or doing the wrong thing. How she had envied Tim his genial social manner which enabled him to mix with people from every stratum, an ability that her relationship with him had shown her she did not possess. She felt alien with his friends, and was unable to relate to his political views and opinion of world events.

Yet their physical attraction for one another had been stronger than their dissimilarities, and as Tim's love for her had deepened and his dependence on her grown, her self-confidence had reasserted itself; not that he was ever aware of her fears and doubts, for she was adept at concealing her innermost feelings.

Tim stirred in her arms, bringing her back to the present. 'You have the most gorgeous eyes,' he whispered, looking into their green depths.

'I was thinking the same about yours,' she smiled as he drew her closer, but resisted him as her closeness made him harden.

'Not again?' she teased, easing away and slipping out of bed.

'Again and again! The more I have you, the more I need you.'

'You're just greedy!'

'Mmm. But at least it doesn't make me fat!' He studied her as she slipped into an emerald silk wrap. The skirt swung round her shapely legs and the tightly cinched belt revealed the contours of her firm, high breasts and small waist. 'All you need to complete the 1920s illusion is a long cigarette holder,' he teased. 'You look like a Scott Fitzgerald heroine.'

Pushing off the duvet, he followed her to the kitchen, grabbing a bathrobe en route. 'I thought we were going to a restaurant?'

'It's a waste of money,' she replied, deftly making a salad before putting a small French bread into the oven to crisp. She hummed to herself as she did so. Sex with Tim always made her feel good.

He watched her for a moment, then methodically set the table and opened the wine. 'For someone who dislikes wasting money,' he grinned, studying the label, 'isn't this extravagant? Or are we celebrating something?'

'I felt like spoiling us,' she replied, and from his pleased expression knew the Australian Shiraz was going to have the effect on him that she desired. But she would wait until he had drunk a couple of glasses before imparting her news.

She put slices of gammon under the grill, then made a four-egg omelette, her movements deft with long practice.

'Get the coffee going, Tim.'

Whistling tunelessly, he did, then set out the cream and gold coffee-cups, a present from his mother. And how like his mother they were! Lindsey thought: elegant, fragile, yet extremely durable if handled carefully. Mrs Ramsden was used to a household of servants, and her two daughters and son had been equally cosseted. Now Tim was roughing it, according to his mother's standards, and no doubt she blamed her daughter-in-law for it, though she had not put her feelings into words.

Discarding the unpleasant thought, Lindsey divided the omelette and gammon into two while Tim took the bread from the oven and poured the wine. The meal was simple but appetising and he did justice to it, though Lindsey, rehearsing how to tell him of her forthcoming trip, merely toyed with her food.

'Not hungry?' he asked.

'Lovemaking has that effect on me,' she said, knowing this would please him, and, seeing it did, she quickly took advantage of it. 'I have to go to Paris for a few days. I was only told today.'

'Not again!' he exploded. 'That's the *second* time in three weeks.'

'It isn't for long,' she placated.

'That's what you said last time, and you were away a week. Do you have to go, Lynnie?'

'Yes. And I wish you wouldn't call me that.'

'Sorry, angel.'

She forced a smile. She hated the abbreviation because it was one her stepfather had used. She had been a scrawny eight-year-old when he had married her mother, but at twelve she had started to bloom, and he had begun hanging around her in a way that had instinctively frightened her. Even now she loathed thinking about it, and had never mentioned it to Tim.

'Why not go down to Evebury while I'm away?' she said aloud, hoping the suggestion would placate him. 'You have several days due.'

'I don't enjoy going without you.'

She knew the reason too well and stifled her irritation. It would have been an opportunity to impress on his parents that he was making his own way, but he obviously couldn't do it unless she was there to give him moral support.

'I can't take my father going on at me to join the business, and mother stoically holding back the tears,' he explained.

Lindsey sniffed. 'Pity they don't realise how happy you are.'

'Happy with *you*, darling, not with my job.'

Morosely Tim pushed back his chair and rose, and she feasted her eyes on him. Tall, slim and strikingly handsome, he had wide shoulders and athletically co-ordinated movements. His face reflected his patrician lineage: high cheekbones, wide forehead, and finely chiselled nose and mouth. His thick, dark blond hair was soft and faintly unruly, and unusually well-shaped eyebrows marked genial grey eyes. With his bathrobe knotted casually around his waist, he epitomised the well-bred man about town.

'Why can't they send someone else to Paris?' he asked. 'You aren't their only researcher.'

'They consider me one of their best,' Lindsey admitted. 'But I promise it will be the last time. I told Grace I don't want to do any more out-of-town interviews.'

'Well, if it's *really* the last time...'

'How was *your* day?' she asked, anxious to change the subject.

'I spent the morning editing Turlow's article and the afternoon finding photographs for him. It's a job anyone with a half-decent education could do. I'm wasting my degree.'

'It would have been equally wasted if you'd gone to work in your family business.'

'I never committed myself to working there.' Tim was instantly on the defensive.

'Your parents took it for granted, and if you hadn't met me I think you'd have joined your father like a shot.'

'Perhaps, but *you're* more important to me than any job.'

'Thank you, but I don't fancy having it on my conscience that you aren't doing what you want.'

'Who the hell *knows* what I want?' he questioned bitterly.

'Well, at least you won't waste your training if you stay on in Fleet Street.'

'As a hack journalist?'

'Give yourself a chance. I'm sure they'll ask you to do Turlow's column when he goes.'

'Is that your ambition for me?' Tim asked slowly. 'To be a political leader writer?'

'What's wrong with it?'

'Nothing. Except it isn't *my* ambition. The thought of spending my life criticising what others have done——'

'And putting forward your own views,' Lindsey intervened silkily. 'Imagine the influence you could have on public opinion.'

'It would be years before anyone listened to me.'

'You have to begin *somewhere*,' Lindsey said irritably. 'Or would you prefer to waste your talent going into the family business and being your father's dogsbody?'

'I'd hardly have been that. It's not a one-man business, you know. It's a sizeable engineering firm, and——' Tim hesitated, then clamped his lips and said no more.

But Lindsey knew what he had held back, and, realising how important it was to clear the air, she finished
the sentence for him.

'And if you don't join your father, he'll eventually
have to sell the company to somebody else, who probably
won't have the same caring attitude to the workforce.'

'Exactly. So what's wrong with that attitude?'

'Nothing. Except that you aren't interested in business,
and your parents shouldn't make you feel guilty because
you don't want to conform to their ideas. That's why
they don't like me. Because they blame me for what they
see as your disloyalty.'

'That isn't true. They don't *blame* you, though I admit
they're upset that I'm not joining Ramsden Engineering.'

Lindsey bit back a sigh. She understood Tim's di-
lemma but didn't see how it could be solved, for if he
toed the line it would mean returning to live in Evebury,
and that would put untold strain on their marriage, for
she knew she would never be happy living there.

'Don't look so upset,' Tim said quickly, his words intimating knowledge of her feelings. 'You're my first
loyalty, darling, and you always will be.' Moving
forward, he caught her round the waist and rubbed his
cheek against hers, his passion, as always, very near the
surface.

Lindsey's breasts swelled at his touch, and she traced
the nape of his neck with her fingertips, fiercely glad to
know that, whatever their difficulties, their love would
always overcome them.

CHAPTER TWO

LINDSEY flung down her pen and stretched her arms lazily above her head, easing her tired muscles. By dint of working long hours she was two days ahead of her schedule, which pleased her because she knew it would delight Tim.

She reached for the telephone, called Air France, and secured a reservation on an early evening flight to London. Replacing the receiver, she picked it up again to call Tim and tell him, then, smiling, put it down. How much nicer to surprise him!

With one eye on the clock, she continued transcribing material from her tape recorder on to her lap-top word processor. She had come to Paris to research the life of a famous French movie star who, twenty years earlier, at the age of forty, had married an out-of-work twenty-year-old French guitarist. Everyone had said it wouldn't last, but they had been proved wrong, for not only were they still blissfully happy, but the guitarist was now one of the most popular musicians in France.

Lindsey knew that Grace Chapman, who was the programme's producer and her immediate boss, would be delighted with the material she had obtained, for she had great aptitude in gathering information, and Grace had recently suggested she would let her appear in a documentary instead of being a backroom girl.

'You have the looks, intelligence and personality to be a presenter,' the woman had stated. 'But telly fame means you'd become a target for every gossip columnist in Fleet Street, and you might not want that.'

'They'd find nothing to gossip about in my life,' Lindsey had replied.

'I'll put your name forward, then.'

15

Since Grace's word carried enormous weight, Lindsey was delighted, yet she had not said a word to Tim, uncertain how would he feel if she suddenly became famous while he was still struggling. Perhaps it might be wiser to soft-pedal her prospects for another year.

Arriving at the airport with time to spare, she wandered into the duty-free shop and, spying Tim's favourite aftershave, which even for her was wickedly expensive, she decided to buy some for him. The bottle she had given him for Christmas was down to the last inch, and she had noticed him using it sparingly.

Deciding in for a penny in for a pound, she also purchased a bottle of champagne as a nice way to mark her earlier than expected return. Tim's favourite brand was Dom Perignon, but the cost was almost double the one she had chosen, and given the amount she had spent on the aftershave it was an extravagance she could ill afford.

Although the flight took only an hour, it was interminable to Lindsey as she envisaged Tim's surprise and pleasure at seeing her. Would they drink the champagne before going to bed, or make love first? When they had been apart for more than a night, he was always impatient to possess her, and as she walked in he would gather her into his arms and carry her into the bedroom, his hunger such that there was no time for foreplay. But she was always wet and ready for him, and their coupling, though swift, was lusty and satisfying.

As her taxi drew to a halt outside the red-brick Edwardian house where they had their apartment, and she saw the light in the sitting-room of their second-floor apartment, she breathed a sigh of relief. Thank goodness Tim was home. In the last half-hour it had occurred to her that her desire to surprise him would backfire if he had gone to the films, or was visiting friends.

Hurrying up the stairs, she quietly unlocked the front door and noiselessly closed it. She wanted Tim's surprise to be total when she walked into the sitting-room.

It certainly was! And a damned unpleasant one too,
for he was on the sofa, locked in a passionate embrace
with a voluptuous blonde.

Staring at them in shocked silence as they swiftly drew
apart, her eyes took in the scene: open hamper stuffed
with goodies in Harrods' distinctive green wrapping, two
glasses beside an empty champagne bottle—Dom
Perignon, to add insult to injury—and black leather
Gucci bag flung carelessly on the floor, beside matching
low-heeled shoes. While the cat's away, the rat did play!
And with no expense spared for his new little sex-kitten!

'Shall I go out and ring the bell?' she finally managed,
tight-lipped.

'It isn't what you imagine,' the girl said.

'Then it's an award-winning imitation!'

'Don't be silly, Lindsey.' Tim's smile was a travesty,
and he avoided her eyes as he began doing up the buttons
of his shirt, which was undone to the waist. 'Patsy is
Peter's sister—the best man at our wedding. Patsy wasn't
there because she was in Australia.'

'I suppose she called in tonight to congratulate you?'
Lindsey's tone was heavily sarcastic as she eyed the girl.

There was no denying she was stunning: silky, corn-
coloured hair falling around slender shoulders, a full
bust, small waist, and nicely rounded hips. As she grace-
fully rose, the long legs exposed by her black kid skirt
were fabulous too.

'Patsy and Peter grew up with me,' Tim was saying.
'Remember me telling you, darling?'

Lindsey had a vague memory of it, and jealousy
mounted as she remembered her mother-in-law saying
she had wanted Tim to marry someone like Patsy Selwyn,
who hailed from a similar background.

'Please don't be angry with Tim,' the girl said now,
in a well-bred drawl. 'This is more my fault than his.'

'It takes two to tango,' Lindsey bit out, throwing her
husband a contemptuous look as he raked his hand
through his tousled hair in an attempt to tidy it.

'What I mean is, I've known Tim most of my life, and when I called him and heard you were away I came over with some food and bubbly—too much bubbly, I guess. That's why——'

'Thanks for the explanation,' Lindsey drawled. 'It's made me feel a lot better.'

Patsy flushed and looked at Tim for help. But none came, and she lost patience. 'For heaven's sake, Lindsey! You're making a mountain out of a molehill.'

'I don't happen to think finding your husband passionately kissing another woman *is* a molehill.'

'But we were a bit tight. It didn't mean a thing. We've known each other for years and——'

'Why don't you just go?' Lindsey cut in wearily. 'And if you think Tim will be faithful to *you*, take him with you!'

Turning on her heels, she walked into the bedroom and slammed the door behind her. As she crumpled on the bed, she heard the front door close, and a moment later Tim came in and put his arms around her.

'Please let me explain, darling,' he murmured. 'Patsy was speaking the truth. I was missing you like hell, and when she offered to come over and keep me company——'

'You decided to use her as my stand-in!' Lindsey shook herself free of him. 'You'd have been in this bed together if I'd arrived an hour later!'

'Don't be crazy! I couldn't make love to anyone except *you*.'

'What were you doing on the sofa—playing patience?'

He shrugged guiltily. 'Things got a little out of hand, I agree, but you're blowing it up out of all proportion.'

'Perhaps I'm not as sophisticated as you,' Lindsey cried. 'But in my world, if a man loves his wife he doesn't make love to someone else the instant her back's turned.' Jumping to her feet, she went to stand by the window. 'I was a fool to work myself into the ground so I could come home earlier than planned. I should have stayed in Paris and lived it up. I had plenty of offers.'

'I'm sure you did,' Tim said softly, from just behind her. 'You're a very beautiful girl.' Catching hold of her shoulder, he swung her round to face him. 'Come to bed, Lindsey, and let me show you how much I love you.'

'The only thing going to bed with me will prove is how horny you are!' she flung at him, furious that he was so insensitive to her mood. Did he think she could discover him in the arms of another woman one moment, and forget about it the next? 'The way I feel right now, I don't want to make love to you ever!'

'For heaven's sake, be reasonable.'

'Reasonable?' Lindsey stormed. 'How reasonable would *you* be if you came home and found me half-naked in another man's arms!'

'I wasn't half-naked,' Tim replied. 'Nor was I making love to Patsy. I was just kissing her. Dammit, I've known her since I was six. Her brother's one of my closest friends.'

'Perhaps you should divorce me and marry *her*! Then you can work for Daddy and live on the family estate instead of in a poky flat on the wrong side of the river!'

'Stop it!' Tim bit out. 'I'm happy here because I'm with *you*, and that's all that matters to me. You should know that by now.'

'Should I?' Lindsey was suddenly gripped with insecurity. 'I don't know anything about you at all.'

Catching the weariness in her voice, he took a tentative step towards her. 'Why don't you get into bed and I'll bring you a hot drink? You look exhausted.'

'Hardly surprising when I've been working flat-out.'

'That's *your* choice.'

'I was talking about Paris!' she snapped. 'I love my job and I can easily cope with it. It was only pressured because I wanted to get home ahead of schedule. Pity I didn't save myself the trouble.'

'For heaven's sake!' Tim's temper rose to meet hers. 'I'm a normal, red-blooded male who was missing his wife and stepped a bit out of line. Stop turning it into the crime of the century.'

'Missing your wife?' Lindsey spluttered. 'Four days without me and you can't control your lust!'

'That wasn't what I meant, and you know it.'

'I certainly do. All I am to you is a good lay, and when I'm not here you'll settle for anyone else!'

'That's a disgusting thing to say.'

'It's the truth!' She was screaming like a harridan yet couldn't stop herself. 'You're sorry you didn't marry Princess Patsy. She's one girl who'd meet with your parents' approval.'

'That's what's bugging you, isn't it? That they don't approve of *you*? Well, why should they?' Tim flung at her harshly. 'You abhor everything they stand for and you've shown them nothing but contempt. You can't bear anyone who's well off, can you?'

'I don't believe in privilege unless it's earned.'

'Dad may have inherited the company from his father, but it's *his* efforts that have made it bigger and more successful.'

'I suppose you resent me because *you* aren't working there too?'

'I don't resent you, Lindsey. You made it plain you wouldn't live in Evebury, so I had no choice. That's the difference between us. You'd have walked away from *me*, but I couldn't have walked away from *you*.'

Dismayed, Lindsey stared at him. Did he genuinely believe what he had just said? Didn't he know how much she loved him? The knowledge that he didn't, hurt her deeply, showing how little he understood her.

'I'm beginning to see why you didn't want to live in Evebury,' Tim went on. 'You were scared you'd lose control over me.'

'Why should I want to control you?'

'Because you have a king-size inferiority complex and it's time you faced it. The main reason you dislike my parents is you're jealous of them. As you're jealous of anyone who has the things you've never had.'

'I was waiting for you to bring up my background,' she cried.

'I never have until now. *You're* always the one bleating about being working class. I don't give a damn where a person comes from. It's what they make of themselves that counts.'

'It's easier to make something of yourself if you start with the advantage of money,' she said scornfully.

'You haven't done so badly,' he retorted.

'Because I chose a profession that recognises ability. What you know instead of whom you know.'

'That applies to most professions these days,' Tim said. 'Face facts, Lindsey, or can't you bear to admit you're wrong?'

'I was wrong to marry *you*,' she flared, not meaning it.

'That's something we can easily rectify,' he rejoined, striding from the room.

'If you walk out now,' Lindsey screamed, 'don't bother coming back.'

'What makes you think I'd want to?'

Before she could answer, the door slammed behind him.

For a long moment she stared at it, then she collapsed on to the dressing-table stool and rested her head in her hands. The evening she had anticipated with such pleasure had turned into a disaster. Tim hadn't meant the things he had said, any more than she had. But words, once spoken, weren't easy to forget. Yet forget them they must, or their marriage was doomed.

Shivering, she undressed, deciding a hot bath might help her unwind. If past arguments were anything to go by, Tim was sure to appear before she had finished and offer to wash her breasts! Her heartbeat quickened. One thing would lead to another, and hurt and anger would fade beneath the stronger force of passion. Not that the reason for their quarrel could be overlooked; too many bitter things had come to the surface for them to be swept aside. But it was better to discuss them when tempers had cooled and realism, rather than emotion, was the arbiter.

But though Lindsey stayed in the bath for ages, Tim did not return, and she finally dried herself and went to bed.

She touched his pillow as she did, and began to cry. Was she really the envious young woman he had accused her of being? She refused to believe it. She had simply wanted him to be independent and not dutifully do his father's bidding. She had assumed he had realised this, but it seemed she was wrong. Resenting his lack of understanding, her anger returned.

Time passed and she lay wakeful, her anger giving way to fear as midnight became two and two became four. Where had he gone? An image of Patsy rose before her, and jealousy brought her upright.

Dammit, she wasn't going to lie awake like this! If Tim thought he could make her jealous he could think again. Storming into the bathroom, she rummaged in the cabinet for a sleeping pill.

Tomorrow, she assured herself, he would return chastened and apologetic, and they would sit down and calmly discuss everything that had taken place tonight. He had behaved stupidly over Patsy, but perhaps the stagnancy of his career, allied to her own burgeoning success, was responsible for it.

But at rock bottom they loved each other, and they must acknowledge this, for it was the cornerstone on which to rebuild their marriage.

CHAPTER THREE

TIM had still not returned when Lindsey finished breakfast next morning.

It was the first time a quarrel between them had lasted so long, and she wondered if she had over-reacted with Patsy. Yet she could not dismiss it as though it had not happened. Her trust in Tim had taken a beating and she needed assuring it would not recur.

Glancing at her watch, and seeing it was after eight-thirty, she gulped down her coffee and dumped her mug and cereal bowl in the sink, then virtuously washed them and put them on the draining rack. At least Tim would find the kitchen spick-and-span when he got back—he hated mess, though he rarely complained. But then he rarely criticised anything; not even the furniture they had purchased second-hand, which she was positive he loathed. But she had adamantly refused to accept anything from his parents' home. The mere sight of an antique chair or valuable rug would have compromised their hard-won independence, and reminded her of the parents-in-law she preferred to forget.

Tim adored his mother, which made it all the more remarkable that he had married a girl she had not liked.

'I'll have to change my accent if you ever decide to become a tycoon!' she had teased him on one occasion.

'Rubbish!' he had grinned. 'With your gorgeous mane of auburn hair and stunning figure, you'll be my greatest asset!'

In fact Lindsey had lost her Midlands twang at university, though she still didn't speak in the plummy tones of Tim's friends. Yet deep down she was the same girl she had always been. Her insecurity was less—Tim's love had lessened it—but it was still there, ready to rise when she felt threatened.

As she had felt last night.

Biting back a sigh, she donned the jacket of her suit and set off to work.

Arriving there, she was told Grace Chapman wanted to see her. It had been an achievement for Lindsey to be taken on as one of her researchers, for it was a post normally given to an experienced person. But Grace had been impressed by her intelligence, and within a few months was sending her out on the most difficult assignments.

'I'm glad you're back from Paris ahead of schedule,' the woman greeted her with a sigh of relief. 'I want you to interview Howard McKay urgently.' She named a renowned biographer of political figures.

'But he lives in Glasgow!'

'If you catch the next shuttle, you can be back tonight.'

As Lindsey was at the door, Grace spoke again.

'Have you considered my offer?'

'About going to America? It sounds marvellous, but I can't accept. I haven't even mentioned it to my husband.'

'I realise six months is a long time,' Mrs Chapman sympathised, 'but it would be invaluable experience for you.'

'I know, and if I'd been single I'd have jumped at it.'

'Think it over again. I'll keep the offer open for another week.'

Returning to her desk, Lindsey realised she had barely an hour to get to the airport. She didn't even have a moment to call Tim. But he was bound to ring her some time today, and she asked Joan Barker, another researcher who shared her office, to explain she had to go to Glasgow unexpectedly, but would be back later that evening.

She reached Howard McKay's home at midday, and was dismayed to find he had gone to the dentist.

'Broke a crown,' his housekeeper explained. 'He said to relax and have a coffee. He shouldn't be long.'

But it was well into the afternoon before the author returned. Tall and thin, he had a craggy, attractive face, and a thatch of grey hair.

'Sorry to have kept you,' he apologised, the teeth he flashed at her bearing witness to the efficiency of his dentist.

Recollecting Mrs Chapman warning her he could be tetchy, Lindsey assured him she hadn't minded waiting to see someone as important as he was. This put him in an excellent humour, and the interview went well.

'Perhaps you'd like to have a look at some of my notes for my latest biography?' he volunteered.

This was a bonus she had not anticipated, and for the next couple of hours she pored over them with him, asking pertinent questions, most of which he didn't answer.

It wasn't until she rose to leave that he invited her to stay to dinner, insinuating he might answer the questions he had previously avoided. Since this would give her interview greater bite, she accepted, giving up hope of flying home that night.

'I'd like to telephone my husband and let him know,' she explained, and was disconcerted when McKay did not offer to leave the room.

In the event it did not matter, for it seemed Tim had not gone to his office today, and she called Joan to see if he had been in touch.

'Afraid not,' Joan answered. 'But if he calls before I leave, do you have a number where he can reach you?'

Lindsey thought quickly. If he rang her here she would not be able to talk freely with Howard McKay listening, and a stilted conversation would do neither of them any good.

'Best not,' she replied. 'Tell him the interview's taken longer than I expected, and I have to stay in Glasgow overnight.' Maybe she could ring Tim from the hotel.

As she set down the receiver, she noticed her host's eyes on her ringless left hand. 'I don't wear jewellery,' she explained.

'A wedding-ring is hardly jewellery. Do you see it as a sign of bondage?'

She shrugged. 'It could be, but not in my case.'

'What does your husband do?'

'He works for Frank Taplow, the political correspondent.'

'He's interested in politics, then?'

'Very,' she lied.

'Do *you* come from a political background?'

Lindsey nearly laughed. 'Hardly. My mother always voted for the best-looking candidate, and my stepfather never voted in his life. From the age of twelve I lived in an orphanage, so my background wasn't a privileged one.'

'Beautiful women make their own background.'

'I prefer to rely on my brains.'

'Most commendable. But if one also has beauty, one has an extra advantage!'

'Spoken like a man,' Lindsey chided. 'But one day soon—when women take their rightful place in world affairs—no man will dare say that!'

Chuckling, McKay rose and extended his arm. 'Shall we go in to dinner?'

It was well after midnight before she booked into a hotel, too late to call Tim, and she ordered an alarm call for six, anxious to catch the earliest shuttle to London. But again fate conspired against her, for the airport was blanketed by fog, and she kicked her heels the entire morning.

Several times she went to call Tim at the newspaper, but each time stopped herself. The more she thought of their quarrel, the wiser it seemed to wait until they were face to face. In the context of her love for him, and their future together, the Patsy episode was best forgiven, though she doubted she could ever forget it.

She had also mulled over his accusations regarding her attitude to his parents, and knew they weren't unjustified. Because of her insecurity, she *was* afraid of their power over him, refusing to see that by marrying her he had shown his independence, and endorsed it further by refusing to join the family firm. So surely she could afford to be less defensive with her in-laws? Perhaps if she made an effort to be nice to them, they would respond in kind.

It was well into the afternoon before she finally reached her office.

'Did Tim call yesterday?' was her first question to Joan.

'About an hour after you rang. He left a number.'

Lindsey looked at it, but it meant nothing to her. Anyway, there was no point calling him there now.

'I'm off,' she announced. 'I left McKay after one this morning, and what with the journey back, I'm whacked.'

Arriving home, she showered and changed into one of her prettiest dresses, then wandered from one room to the other, nervous as a girl waiting for her first date.

It was only as she decided to have a cup of coffee that she saw her breakfast cup and saucer on the draining board where she had left them yesterday morning. Odd that Tim hadn't put them away. His tidiness was something she teased him about. When he had learned she was remaining in Glasgow for the night, he must have stayed over wherever he had gone.

She rummaged in her bag for the number Joan had given her, started to dial it, then, on an impulse, went over to the desk for Tim's address book. Leafing through it, she could find no number corresponding to the one she had, and she went into the hall for the telephone directory.

With trembling fingers she picked up the L to Z. Yes, there was a P. Selwyn listed and the number tallied with the one Joan had given her. Did the 'P' stand for Patsy or Peter? There was one way to find out, and she took it.

She hardly remembered the cab ride to Knightsbridge, and was in a cold sweat when she reached the entrance of a luxury apartment block near Harrods. There was an entry-phone at the door but she was reluctant to use it, unwilling to warn Patsy—if it was her and not her brother—that she was here.

After what seemed an age but was only a moment, a well dressed couple emerged, and she slipped past them into the foyer. Luckily the porter was talking to another resident, and Lindsey darted into the lift.

Apartment twelve was on the top floor, and her heart was thudding madly as she rang the bell. Footsteps sounded on parquet, then the door was flung open and Patsy stared at her, dumbfounded.

'Good lord, *you*!'

'Is Tim here?'

'He's in Evebury.'

Lindsey was taken aback. 'But he—he's stayed here the last two nights, hasn't he?'

'Yes,' Patsy said, 'and frankly I don't blame him. If you were childish enough to throw him out, what did you expect?'

Lindsey felt sick. How could Tim discuss their quarrel with the girl who was the cause of it? Didn't he realise how disloyal it was, or didn't he care?

'I was angry,' she said, then wondered why she should excuse her behaviour to Patsy. Without another word she turned and ran down the stairs.

Her worst suspicions had been confirmed. After their quarrel, Tim had spent the night with Patsy, and had done so again when she had been stuck in Glasgow. Lindsey tried to assure herself that they might have slept in separate rooms, but she could not believe it. Bearing in mind that he had had no qualms about kissing the girl while his wife was in Paris, it was difficult to imagine he had only gone to Patsy's apartment for tea and sympathy!

Ignoring the taxis that passed by, Lindsey strode along the hard, unyielding pavements, and by the time she reached home the soles of her feet were burning. No swift, silent lift here to whisk her to a luxury apartment; just steep stairs, with each landing exuding its own distinctive smell. Lavender water from the elderly woman who had originally owned the house before converting it, dog from the Coopers, whose Basset hound was not house-trained, and nothing from their floor, Lindsey realised miserably as she reached her front door, and for once would have welcomed the aroma of Tim's burnt cooking.

Desolated, she went straight to the kitchen to make a cup of tea. The working class panacea, she thought wryly. Patsy would no doubt have poured herself a glass of champagne.

To hell with Patsy and what she would have done! Lindsey sat down at the kitchen table and waited for the water to boil. Tim's departure for Evebury meant only one thing: he was leaving London to join the family company. She was hurt that he had not seen fit to talk it over with her first. Was it because he wanted to prove he was his own man?

Angrily she poured boiling water over her teabag and some of it splashed on her hand. With a cry she put down the kettle, the shock of the scald shattering her frayed nerves.

Tears streaming down her face, she ran into the living-room and flung herself on to the sofa. Her life was over. At the first trouble between them Tim had fled to his family like a chicken to its coop. Lindsey felt as though a door had been slammed in her face, leaving her broken, crushed, and completely alone.

CHAPTER FOUR

THE piercing ring of the telephone at her side roused Lindsey from her stupor, and dazedly she reached for the receiver, sitting up swiftly as she heard Tim at the other end.

'Why haven't you called me?' he said curtly. 'Didn't you get my message?'

'Yes. But I didn't return from Glasgow till late this afternoon. I understand you're at Evebury?'

'Yes, I am. So you rang the number I left?'

'I went there,' she said as casually as she could. It was pointless not telling him, given that Patsy would.

He was silent, as if surprised, and Lindsey's resentment became savage. 'So you've gone back to Mummy and Daddy?'

'Dammit, Lindsey, I'm here because——'

'You were tired of pigging it with me!'

'We weren't exactly starving in a garret!' he responded irritably. 'My father's had a stroke and is in hospital.'

Lindsey was shocked into silence.

'Will you come down?' Tim asked.

'Is he...how serious is it?'

'Thank God it wasn't a severe one. The specialist says he should recover completely. But it was totally unexpected.'

'These things often are.' Lindsey was surprised to find her voice husky. 'Please give him my best wishes.'

'Does that mean you won't be coming here?'

'There isn't much point, is there? Your heart's in Evebury and mine's in London.' She had a sudden inspiration. 'Not for much longer, though. I'm going to America for six months.'

30

'You can't be serious!' Tim exclaimed.

'Yes, I am. Grace offered me the chance a few weeks ago and I've finally decided to accept it. It's for the best.'

'The best for whom? If you're going because of Patsy, you're mad!'

'Mad because I can't be as sophisticated about it as you?' Lindsey stormed back, longing for him to say he was sorry and that he loved her more than anyone in the world.

But he said none of these things, his tone icy as he spoke. 'You're making too much of something that's totally unimportant and——'

'I consider it bloody important!'

'I'm in no mood to plead with you, Lindsey. Do what the hell you like. You always have, anyway. But I'll say one thing for you—you certainly choose your moments!'

'Our marriage was a mistake and the other night proved it.'

'Stop using Patsy as an excuse,' Tim exploded. 'You've obviously been looking for one from the moment you were offered the job in the States. And if that's what you want—go!'

The receiver was crashed down, and Lindsey drew a shaky breath and returned to the kitchen. She was trembling as though with fever, and she forced herself to make another cup of tea and a cheese sandwich, then sat in an armchair and watched a programme she had researched a month ago.

But for all the attention she paid to it it might as well have been in Chinese. All she could think of was Tim, and the lie she had told him. Should she call back and admit she'd no sooner leave him for six months than fly to the moon? Or was it better to go to Evebury and do it in person? It was probably the surest way of repairing their quarrel.

Lindsey glanced at her watch. It was eight-thirty, too late to catch a train now—and Tim had taken the car so she could not drive down. She would have to wait until tomorrow. By then, he'd have realised he had over-reacted and ring to apologise.

When morning dawned with no word from him, her anger resurfaced. Why should *she* be the one to patch things up, when it was his behaviour that had caused their row? Their marriage had been far from smooth, and *he* might have been looking for a pretext to end it. If so, Patsy had provided the perfect solution, for he would blame their parting on her jealousy—brought on by her inferiority complex!

If that was the case, she *would* go to the States.

She told Grace Chapman of her decision as soon as she arrived at the office.

'I'm delighted,' the woman said. 'It's a marvellous career move for you. And your husband doesn't mind?'

'No,' Lindsey lied, the implication of all she was saying suddenly overwhelming her. 'I can leave at the end of the week if you wish,' she added.

'Marvellous. I'll notify New York.'

The next few days were filled with preparations for her departure. Lindsey still hoped to hear from Tim, and worried how to tell Grace that she didn't want to go to New York after all. But though she rushed to answer the telephone when it rang, it was never Tim at the other end, and she gradually accepted that she wouldn't hear from him.

Although she had had little contact with her father-in-law, she contacted the hospital to see how he was getting on, pleased to learn he was going home at the end of the week.

On the Thursday night before her departure she hardly slept, tossing and turning as she debated what to do. Her marriage might have reached an impasse, but that didn't mean it was over. She and Tim could use her stay in America as a cooling-off period, and given goodwill on both sides they could get back together on her return. She would tell him this before leaving; it was the adult way to handle the situation.

Having reached this conclusion, she was on tenter-hooks to speak to him, but controlled her agitation until eight a.m., when she deemed the Ramsden household to be awake.

To her surprise the telephone was instantly answered by her mother-in-law, making her realise that the family were still on the alert regarding Mr Ramsden.

'I'm sorry to bother you,' Lindsey said after the usual polite greetings had been mouthed, 'but may I have a word with Tim?'

'He's already left for the factory. Can I give him a message?'

'No, thank you. I'll call him there.'

'I doubt if you'll get him. He went in early to collect some papers before going on to an appointment.'

'Do you know where? I *must* talk to him.'

'Hold on a moment, I'll ask Patsy. She spoke to him before he left the house.'

Patsy! So she was there with him! If Lindsey had har-boured a secret hope of a last-minute reconciliation, it was shattered now.

'Don't bother,' she said quickly. 'Don't—don't even tell him I called.'

'Are you sure?'

'Yes,' Lindsey answered. 'I—er—I'm glad to hear Mr Ramsden is coming home this weekend.'

'You know?' There was surprise in her mother-in-law's voice, and Lindsey guessed that Tim had told her they had quarrelled.

'I called the hospital to see how he was,' she ex-plained, and before Mrs Ramsden had a chance to say anything else she hung up, her sense of despair turning to fury as she thought of Patsy.

Going into the bedroom, she finished her packing. The apartment was in Tim's name so he could dispose of it as he chose. Clearly Patsy was remaining in his life; having lost him once, she wasn't going to let him get away again.

Lindsey stared round the room, her eyes brimming with tears as her glance fell on the bed where she and Tim had made such passionate love. Unbidden, she recalled some of the happy incidents in their life together: Tim teaching her to water-ski on their honeymoon and both of them tumbling into the water; the pancakes he had determined to cook for her birthday breakfast, the first one tossed so high it had stuck to the ceiling! So much to laugh over, so many tender moments to remember.

She shook her head. Nostalgia would get her nowhere. Their marriage was over—for the time being at least, she qualified instantly—and she had to concentrate on the next six months.

But first she had to write to Tim. Plenty *needed* saying, but face to face, not cold-bloodedly in a letter. If only his father hadn't been taken ill... If only he didn't have to be at Evebury... If only she could relive this last week...

In despair, Lindsey finally put pen to paper.

As you know, I'll be in New York for the six months, though if I do well I may be asked to stay longer.

I enclose my share of last quarter's gas, electricity and telephone bills, but if I owe you for anything else, please let me know. I'm not sure where I'll be staying, but the office will forward any letters.

Firmly she signed her name. She had been deliberately ambiguous, leaving Tim to read into her note as little or as much as he liked. Sealing the envelope, she went out at once to post it, afraid that if she didn't she might change her mind and remain in England.

Lindsey was swept off her feet by the frenetic atmosphere of New York. Everything was larger than life here, and moved at breakneck speed, so that nothing seemed permanent, not even emotions—and that suited her fine.

For the first few weeks she was booked into a small hotel, courtesy of Universal TV, but before the month was out she was sharing an apartment near Fifth Avenue with Mary Brompton, another girl working as a researcher. Mary was New York born and bred, and she quickly introduced Lindsey to the city, and made her feel at home.

Lindsey's day started earlier than in London, and she was always at the office by eight. Her particular project was to collect material for a documentary series on immigrants and their influence on the country's culture, which was being co-financed by a big American network. The research was exhaustive, and she often stayed late collating it. It left her little free time, other than at weekends, and with Mary's help these were soon fully occupied.

Museums, art galleries, concerts, theatre, movies—Lindsey enjoyed them all, as she also did the mind-boggling choice of ethnic restaurants and discount clothing stores! But though her social life flourished, Tim kept intruding into her thoughts. What was he doing? Was he still with Patsy? More important, was he wondering the same thing about *her*?

She spent hours remembering their whirlwind courtship. Though she had not considered herself a romantic, she had been delighted with the white rose delivered to her room at college each day. There was also perfume, books of poetry, and a gold bracelet with a single, 'I love you' charm. She had frequently protested at his extravagance, but he had assured her he could afford it, and how better to spend his money than on the girl he loved? It was sad to admit how short a time his love had lasted.

In spite of the lifeline she had offered in her letter to him, he had not attempted to contact her. It was as if he wished to sever their relationship completely, and even the cheques she had left for him remained uncashed.

Would their relationship have succeeded if they had settled in Evebury and Tim had gone into the family business? Yet, if he had, her own career would not have taken off, and the independent girl Tim had fallen for would have disappeared. No, she reflected, whatever way they had played it, given their respective backgrounds their life together had been doomed from the start.

Eventually she would forget him; at least sufficiently to consider another relationship. But unfortunately the men who appealed to her were all Tim lookalikes, though none of them had his charm, and she was never tempted to launch into an affair.

A month before she was due to return to England, Phil Marsham, Grace Chapman's American counterpart, asked if she was interested in remaining in New York.

'For how long?' she enquired, gratified by the compliment but unwilling to risk losing her position in the London company.

'For as long as you like.'

'I'm tired of doing research. Grace said I could front some of the shows when I went back.'

'Stay here and you can front them all.'

This had been her goal for the future, but she had not envisaged grasping it so soon. 'You mean that? You're not just holding out a carrot?'

'Sure it's a carrot—but it's yours to eat!'

'Then I'll stay!' Lindsey beamed.

Later that evening she wrote to tell Tim of her plans.

In spite of its down side, New York's a great city and I enjoy living here. I'm sure you're managing very well without me, and I'll understand if you wish to make our separation permanent.

Here she paused, wondering if she was being too brief, too final. She thought not. She had stated the facts as she saw them, and if he didn't agree he was free to say so. Damn him, he'd said nothing since the day she had left London. Not a call, not a card.

A week later she had a stilted reply saying he was in no hurry for a divorce, and preferred to wait the statutory two years, when it would be granted with the minimum of fuss. If she wanted one sooner, she would have to furnish the necessary evidence herself.

Furiously she flung his letter aside. What a nerve! Did he think she was born yesterday? If she needed evidence to divorce him, she'd cite Patsy. Yet deep down she knew she wouldn't. Not unless she fell so madly in love with someone else that she wanted to marry them immediately, about as likely as pigs flying, in her present emotional state. No, she'd play it as coolly as Tim, and if he was content to wait, so was she.

With great determination Lindsey began building a new life. She was happy to stay for the foreseeable future; certainly her career would move forward at a faster pace than if she returned home.

Quite how fast it *did* go took her by surprise, for three months after accepting Phil's offer she researched, produced, and appeared in her own documentary. The ratings were excellent, and to show their appreciation Universal TV gave her a bonus, large enough for her to rent an empty apartment of her own. She filled it with pieces bought from the numerous second-hand stores that flourished in the city, and was pleased by the admiring comments from friends at the William-Morris-papered walls, polished wood floorboards scattered with rugs, and delicate sprigged fabrics on the squashy sofas.

'You've created an English-country-house look in the heart of New York!' they exclaimed.

It had been a totally unconscious act, but once it was brought to her attention she realised that the country house she had unconsciously copied was Ramsden Manor!

A burgeoning bank account brought other advantages too. When money was tight she had given little thought to clothes, but now she no longer had to skimp she discovered she had an excellent eye for what suited her, and her tall, graceful body was shown to advantage in the elegantly casual look of Ralph Lauren and Armani.

For the next two years Lindsey did all she could to forget the past, but it came forcibly back to her during her second summer in New York when she picked up an English newspaper one morning—left in the office by a visiting British VIP—and read that Ramsden Engineering had been bought out by Semperton Trust, a large company with its fingers in many different businesses.

So Tim's joining the family firm had not saved it! What a blow it must have been to his pride. Still, he was young enough to build another career for himself. It was his father for whom she felt sympathy, for he would find it difficult to start something new in his mid-fifties, yet was too young to settle for retirement.

She read on, and was glad she had done so, for it appeared that Mr Ramsden's aggressive price-cutting in the past year had caused blood to be spilt in Semperton's engineering arm, and the best way of stemming it, according to the article, was to 'invite the enemy on board'.

Lindsey couldn't help smiling. Tim's father had always been kind to her, though fairly remote—a fact which she had put down to his wife—and she was pleased that he wasn't going to be put out to pasture. Crumpling the newspaper, she tossed it into the bin, wishing she could as easily toss out the memories of Tim that came crowding into her brain.

'It's over,' she said aloud. 'I've made a new life for myself and you have no part in it.'

'You calling me?' her assistant enquired, putting her head round the door.

'No. Just reminding myself of something important.'

Another year went by and, aware that for the past twelve months Tim could have obtained a divorce with the minimum of fuss, she waited for his lawyer to write and say it had come through. When he didn't, she was puzzled. Surely Tim wanted his freedom, given that he had made no move towards a reconciliation? Not that she'd have him back anyway; she still resented his apathy, his total lack of caring.

By the fourth year his image had blurred, and it was as if he belonged to another life; one she recalled with neither pain nor pleasure, only numbness.

Around this time Phil Marsham and his wife invited her out to celebrate their wedding anniversary. She dressed for the evening in a body-hugging cream silk suit, its simplicity suiting her tall, slender figure. Her free-tumbling curls were long since gone, replaced by a silky auburn swath brushed back from her face to fall smoothly to just below her ears.

Everything about her today was sophisticated, though many of her friends thought her too thin. Yet this emphasised her beautiful bone-structure, throwing her high cheekbones into relief, and drawing attention to her full red mouth and luminous green eyes.

Lowering her head, she fastened the clasp of her chunky gold necklace and matching bracelet. Strange that she, who had once scorned jewellery, should today regard it as part of her persona. Grabbing a light wrap and small Chanel purse, she went down to the foyer, where Phil was waiting.

He was a wiry man of medium build and height. Yorkshire by birth, though no one would have guessed it from his accent which, after twenty years in the States with an American wife, had become authentically New York.

'The one person I know who's always punctual,' he greeted her. 'Belle's waiting in the car.'

'I was going to suggest you both come up for a drink.'

'I can't face the aggro of parking. Besides, Robert Lawson's meeting us at Rico's in ten minutes.'

Rico's she knew of—it was a chic restaurant on the East Side—but Robert Lawson she had difficulty placing, though the name rang a bell.

'Should I know him?' she asked as they went outside.

'Think of mega-bucks and take-overs.'

Lindsey stopped in her tracks. '*That* Lawson!'

'None other.'

'How come you know him?'

'What an unflattering question to put to your boss!' Phil tried to look pained, and she laughed.

'Don't give me that. You're the most confident man I know.'

'Because I'm a happy one. Happy in my job, happy in my marriage. I'd like that for *you*.'

'Right now I'm happy to settle for my job.' Quickly she changed the subject. 'So how come Lawson is honouring you with his company?'

'We grew up in the same village near Manchester. Plus the fact that he likes to maintain a high profile, and I'm willing to help him if you think there may be a story in it for us. We'll know better when we find out what he's shopping around for in the States.'

'I thought it was going to be an anniversary celebration for only the three of us,' Lindsey teased as she joined Belle in the back seat. 'Now it turns out to be a business dinner!'

'Don't you know Phil?' his wife sighed. 'Fifty years from now he'll be organising business dinners for St Peter!'

Lindsey laughed. As a top television executive, Phil met most of the leading personalities visiting New York, and within weeks of starting to work for him she had been caught up in his frantic social activity. Not surprisingly, given her stunning looks, she was propositioned with unremitting frequency, but she had developed enough poise to keep all would-be lovers at bay without offending them.

'What's Robert Lawson like as a person?' she asked Phil.

'Belle will tell you.'

Lindsay turned to her.

'A self-made millionaire, who makes no pretence about it,' Belle said. 'He's tough but charming, and would be death as a husband, though I think he'd be great as a lover.'

'What category am I in?' Phil enquired.

'Both!'

Belle's description of Robert Lawson might be right, Lindsey mused as they entered the restaurant and he rose from his table to greet them. In his late thirties, with glinting brown eyes marked by heavy brows as dark as his thick, curly black hair, he was a big man with a well-proportioned body: wide shoulders, broad chest tapering to slim hips, large hands with carefully manicured nails, and bronzed skin that had the cared-for look that went with a first class fitness club.

'So you're Lindsey,' he murmured as, introductions made, she sat beside him. 'Have you deserted England for good?'

'I'm not sure. At the moment I love my work too much to consider going home.'

'It is only your work that keeps you here?'

Knowing what he meant, she gave him an innocent look. 'There's Angus, of course.'

'Of course,' he said smoothly. 'I thought you might have someone special. He sounds a Scot.'

'Siamese, as it happens.'

For an instant he was taken aback, then he chuckled. 'A cat! You caught me there, my dear.' He eyed her speculatively. 'I'd have thought you more the Saluki type.'

'I'm not sure whether to be flattered by that,' she said. 'I always associate them with well-bred idleness!'

'I associate them with elegance and beauty,' he replied softly.

Aware of the amused looks passing between Belle and Phil, Lindsey resolved to keep the conversation general, and as if aware of her intention Robert Lawson did the same. He was an excellent raconteur, and listening to his stories—which were mainly political—she began to feel homesick.

It was not until they left the restaurant and were waiting for Phil's car to be brought to them, that Robert quietly asked if she was free to have dinner with him the following evening.

'I'll have to check my diary,' she said equally quietly.

'Is that a polite turn-down?'

'It means I have to check my diary.' Her voice was devoid of expression. 'I have a heavy week.'

'I'll call you in the morning,' he said, shepherding both women to the car.

They did not talk again, and he allowed Phil to accompany her to the door when they reached her apartment block, which would have piqued her had not feminine intuition told her he had behaved this way to exploit the abrasive quality in his personality, an abrasiveness that she was sure attracted many women.

But did it attract her? Not at the moment. All she knew was that he was as different from Tim as chalk from cheese, and that, she reflected as she closed her apartment door and went into her bedroom, might be the reason why she would go out with him tomorrow night.

CHAPTER FIVE

'MR LAWSON phoned twice,' her secretary announced as Lindsey came into the office next morning. 'He left a number for you to call.'

Lindsey was surprised by his keenness. Smiling, she dialled, and he picked up the phone himself.

'I thought you'd be at the office bright and early,' he greeted her, his voice deeper than she remembered it. 'Have you checked your diary?'

'Yes, I'm free.'

'Good. I'm staying at Bedford House, Park Avenue. Apartment eleven. I'll expect you at seven-thirty.'

The line went dead and she gave a gasp of astonishment. What cheek! Ordering her to call for him as if she were his personal assistant.

'Anything wrong?' her secretary asked.

Lindsey shook her head. Maybe she was being childish. Robert Lawson probably had a tight schedule and shouldn't be judged by normal standards.

Despite her irritation, she arrived on time at his apartment that evening.

When she refused a second drink, he suggested they leave for dinner and, expecting him to take her to a restaurant where he might possibly make an item in a gossip column next day, he surprised her by taking her to Mr Albert's, a discreet dining club in an elegant brownstone house.

'Have you been here before?' he asked as they were immediately shown to their table. Mr Albert's guests did not sit at the bar drinking with strangers!

'Yes.' Lindsey was glad she could answer affirmatively. She didn't want Robert thinking only *he* could take her somewhere special. 'The head of a rival network

43

brought me here last month to try to bribe me away from Universal.'

'Did you accept?'

'No. Doing a chat show isn't my scene. I believe the documentaries we do are worthwhile.'

'So you turned down fame and fortune for——'

'Job satisfaction,' she cut in abruptly.

To his credit, Robert instantly saw she was in no mood to be taken lightly. 'I can appreciate that. Job satisfaction means everything to me too. The day I decide I no longer enjoy the cut and thrust of business, I'll sell out and retire.'

'Sell out? Wouldn't you prefer to appoint someone to take over from you?'

'I'd be watching him like a hawk to make sure he carried on the company the way I would. And nobody is as good as I am. That's why, when I've had enough, I'll give up completely.'

'Are you always so modest?' Lindsey couldn't help asking.

'I believe in being honest. I started with nothing and now have one of the biggest engineering companies in the country. I'm negotiating to buy another one, and if I can persuade them to sell it to me I'll be *the* biggest.'

'Which is the biggest at the moment?'

'Semperton Engineering. It's a part of Semperton Trust. A damn octopus that has its tentacles into everything.'

Lindsey wondered whether to tell him that they had bought her father-in-law's engineering company a few years ago. Indeed, only last week she had read a flattering article about him in *Time* magazine, saying that Semperton Trust rated his business acumen so highly that they had just elected him chairman and managing director of the main board; a remarkable achievement for a man who had only come into the organisation three years ago.

As she opened her mouth to speak, the waiter presented them with the menu, and by the time they had chosen their meal, she decided that she didn't know Robert Lawson well enough to disclose anything about her private life.

'Let's not talk any more about me,' he said as their first course was set before them. 'Tell me about yourself. You've been married, I believe. I asked Phil, and he couldn't evade a blunt question.'

'You could have waited to ask *me*.'

'You seemed to have some doubts about seeing me, and I wanted to know what I was up against.'

'And do you?'

'I think so. You've been hurt once and have put up your guard. It's usual when a person has been divorced.'

'Are you speaking from experience?'

He shook his head. 'Until recently I've been too busy building my fortune to have time to build a private life.' He set down his fork. 'How long have you been free?'

'I'm not. I'm still married.' She was pleased to see he looked put out at being wrong-footed. 'Didn't Phil tell you that too?'

'No. He said as little as possible.' A blunt-fingered hand, the nails well kept, rubbed the side of his face. 'Look, it's no crime to be curious about you. If we'd met in London I'd have played it differently, but I'm not here long and——'

'I'm flattered,' Lindsey cut in. The poor man had suffered enough for his curiosity, and she genuinely was flattered by his interest. 'Are you always so inquisitive about the women you date?'

'Only when they're as beautiful and bright as you.' He leaned towards her. 'Are you hoping to get back with your husband?'

He was blunt all right! No one had asked her this, and she found it painful to answer. Yet perhaps there was catharsis in pain.

'My marriage is over. We've just been rather dilatory in making it official.'

Robert pursed his lower lip. It drew her attention to his mouth, which was well shaped but thin. 'Is your husband in entertainment too?'

'No. I'm not sure what he's doing at the moment. We met in Cambridge, married soon after we graduated and split ten months later.'

'So he's the same age as you?'

Lindsey shook her head, her silky hair falling forward as she did. In the subdued lighting it was Titian red—the deep colour of vintage claret. 'He's six years older. He went to Ethiopia with Voluntary Service Overseas before going to Cambridge. He also skied a lot.'

'Sounds as if he has a monied background.'

She shrugged. 'You didn't, I take it?'

'Too true!'

'Me neither.'

'So we've something in common,' Robert stated. 'And we both have reason to be proud of ourselves.'

'You more than me. I may work for a big company, but you *own* one!'

'Don't underrate yourself, Lindsey. Your documentaries make an impact on the way people think. And that's very important.' He leaned closer to her. 'I have to go to Washington for the next few days, but I'll see you when I get back.'

'I can't promise,' she murmured, irritated by his presumption.

'I'll keep hoping. You have to relax some time.'

She made no comment, and he signalled for the bill.

It wasn't until they were in a taxi on the way to her home that he referred to her reluctance to see him.

'Why don't you like me, Lindsey?'

'I—er—why do you think that?'

'Your unwillingness to fix a firm date to see me again.'

'I said I might be busy. But if I'm free I'll be pleased to go out with you.'

'Pleased? Can't you do better than that?'

'I don't think you need encouragement.'

'Usually I don't,' he confessed with fetching candour, and fell silent as the taxi stopped outside her apartment block. 'I'll see you to the door,' he said, jumping out.

'It isn't necessary.'

'I'm doing it out of pleasure, not necessity!'

They reached the glass entrance, and pulling her gently round to face him, he brushed his lips across hers. His touch was soft, his mouth warm, and Lindsey found herself liking it.

'I'll call you,' he said as he drew back and, touching her cheek lightly, returned to the waiting taxi.

With his footsteps receding in her ears, Lindsey put her key in the lock, her body tingling with an excitement she hadn't felt in years.

CHAPTER SIX

NEXT day Lindsey found herself pleasantly anticipating Robert's call, and was disappointed when he rang to say he wouldn't be returning from Washington till after the weekend.

'Why not join me here for a few days?' he suggested.

'It's impossible.'

'Am I back of the class again?'

'Of course not. But I don't like being rushed.'

'What choice do I have? I'm here for four weeks, and for half of them I'll be on the West Coast.'

'You can always write to me,' she teased.

'Oh, sure,' he grunted. 'Boss of Lawson and Briggs writes love-letters to married woman. I can see the headlines!'

Speechless at the implied accusation, Lindsey quietly set the telephone back on its hook.

An hour later three dozen yellow tea-roses arrived for her; the card accompanying it was written in flowing American script, though the message was pure Robert.

'Again I've put my foot in it. Forgive me.'

Lindsey carried the flowers into the outer office and dumped them on her secretary's desk. 'Do what you like with these. I'm also unavailable if Mr Lawson calls.'

'All day?'

'Every day.'

Hardly had the words left her lips than he was on the line, and leaving her secretary mouthing excuses Lindsey returned to her office.

It wasn't easy to work, for her anger was still vibrant. She wasn't being thin-skinned, she assured herself; she had every justification to be furious with Robert. His remark had been crass in the extreme. Tim wouldn't have—oh, lord, there she went again—comparing every man with Tim.

Of course *he* wouldn't have made such a comment. After all, who'd want to compromise Tim, living contentedly in Evebury? Or had he moved back to London when Ramsden Engineering was taken over by Semperton's? Whatever, she couldn't imagine him behaving as crudely as Robert.

Yet in mitigation of what Robert had said, she had to admit he was in the public eye and, as such, there would always be people more than happy to bring him down. Yet to think she might be one of them... She shook her head, disappointed by his poor judgement.

Arriving home, she found the entrance to her apartment blocked by half a dozen baskets of flowers, all bearing cards with the same two words: 'Forgive me'.

Could she? She was still uncertain, wondering whether his sharp comment had been the result of having had his fingers burned by some wily woman in the past. She hadn't thought of that till now, but it made sense.

Unlocking her door, she carried the flowers inside. It was a good thing she didn't have to arrange them in vases! She couldn't help smiling at the thought, and at the same time was aware of her hurt lifting.

Hardly had she brought in the last basket when Robert rang.

'At least you're willing to speak to me,' he said without preamble.

'You don't deserve it.'

'Right. It was crass of me. But there was a reason I——'

'You once had your fingers burned?'

'Not mine. A close friend, and it destroyed him. But it still doesn't excuse what I said to you. Hell! It's frustrating apologising on the telephone. Are you sure you can't fly down even for one evening?'

Lindsey was tempted but resisted it. 'Angus dislikes being left alone all night.'

Angus, hearing his name, emitted a loud scream to show he was impatient for his dinner.

'What's that noise?' Robert demanded.

'A Siamese request for liver and a saucer of milk.'

'You mean you really do have a cat? I thought you were joking.'

'I never joke about Angus,' Lindsey said in hurt tones. 'He's very sensitive.'

'I wish you cared as much for *my* feelings. I don't fancy a cat as a rival!'

'Don't flatter yourself!'

He chuckled. 'If I can alter my schedule, I'll come back Sunday. If not, have dinner with me Monday?'

She agreed without looking at her diary, but when Sunday came and went with no courtesy call to say he couldn't make it, she wished she had not promised to see him the next night. What was there about the man that got under her skin? she wondered for the tenth time. He wasn't the type who usually appealed to her. Could that be the attraction? That he was so different from Tim that she wouldn't be tempted to compare them?

Irritated, yet sad as thoughts of Tim conjured up the past, she poured herself a glass of wine to lighten her mood. She had heard no news of him since they had parted, not even in letters from her friends. But of course her friends hadn't been his, and would think they were doing her a favour by not mentioning him.

At midnight, as she was getting into bed, Robert telephoned.

'Sorry I couldn't make it tonight. It was impossible to get away.'

'It doesn't matter.'

'I'm sorry you said that. It mattered to *me*. Is it still on for tomorrow?'

'Why should you think it isn't?'

'Because you're an unpredictable young woman,' he said, and hung up.

It wasn't true she was unpredictable, she thought as she turned off the light. Trouble was, Robert was used to getting his own way and resented wasting time on the preliminaries. In the past four years many men had tried to get her into bed, and several times she had almost succumbed, but memory of Tim had prevented her entering a new relationship. Only now had she begun to tire of her bachelor girl existence, and long to love and be loved.

Languidly, she closed her eyes and drifted into sleep, thinking of Robert's dark, sensual looks and powerful body. But it was of Tim she dreamed, his light brown hair kissed gold by the sun, his hands gentle upon her skin, his mouth warm and demanding on hers. Filled with desire, her legs parted to give him entry, but he floated away and she ran after him, crying herself into wakefulness.

For a brief second she remained locked in her dream, then she turned on her side and burst into tears; not the bitter tears of the first days of their parting, but tears for the loss of innocence, for the naïve girl who had believed in the sanctity of marriage vows and lasting love.

Monday evening brought Robert and dinner at another chic restaurant. As if to show he trusted her, his account of his meetings with various senators and top executives was amusingly indiscreet, and he did not make the mistake of saying it was 'off the record'.

Next day he left for the West Coast, and she confidently waited to hear from him, but five days lapsed before she did, and she was disconcerted by her pleasure at hearing his deep, slow voice.

'I went unexpectedly on a trek to Colorado,' he announced. 'It was a stag party with everyone trying to prove they were one of the boys.'

'Were you?'

'Right down to the shorts and sneakers!' Hearing her laugh, he caught her mood. 'Missed me?'

'Very much.'

His silence showed she had taken him by surprise. 'I've so much to say to you, I don't know where to begin,' he said finally. 'It will have to wait till I see you.' In his predictably abrupt fashion, he hung up.

Lindsay smiled, aware of a burgeoning excitement at the prospect of seeing him. Seven more days until he returned. It was a pity she couldn't occupy herself with work, but the summer season was under way and no further documentaries were planned till October. During this time she usually took a well-earned break, but in her present mood she was uncertain where to go. A trip to England was a no-no, for Robert would think she was chasing him!

The following day she went to see her travel agent, returning home still undecided between three months on a ranch in Montana or discovering her artistic soul in Sante Fe!

After a leisurely bath, Santa Fe beckoned invitingly, and preparing for it she donned a colourful jade-green nightgown and matching négligé—last year's Christmas present from Phil and Belle—let her hair fall in a riot of curls to her shoulders, instead of blowdrying it into its usual sleek style, and settled on the sofa with Angus purring on her stomach.

A ring at the doorbell startled her to her feet, and she tiptoed into the vestibule to peer through the peephole. Robert! A rush of desire, as pleasant as it was unexpected, ran through her as she undid the safety chain and lock.

In a dark grey suit, he was larger than she remembered him. He dwarfed the small hall and she stepped back, smiling. Neither of them spoke for a moment, then he pulled her into his arms and began kissing her: fierce, demanding kisses that required submission rather than response.

'I've wanted to do that from the moment I set eyes on you,' he muttered thickly upon her mouth, and kissed her again.

This time his lips were gentler and she kissed him back, enjoying the feel of his mouth, the warmth of being close to his body. But as his tongue edged between her lips she pulled away and led him into the sitting-room.

'Surprised to see me?' he asked.

'Very.'

'I couldn't stay away. I have to return tomorrow, but——'

'You came back for *one night*?'

'The way I feel I'd have come for one hour!' He wrapped his arms around her. 'I want you so much...'

His hands curved round her buttocks and pressed her close to him as he kissed her eyelids, the soft skin behind her ears, the delicate line of her shoulder. His head lowered to her breasts and she could not restrain a nervous shiver; it was years since a man had kissed her this intimately, and she couldn't abandon herself to Robert's touch. With a little cry she pushed him away.

'Why?' he questioned.

'Would you believe I'm scared?' She moved to the sofa, but stopped abruptly. 'What a hostess I am! May I offer you a drink?'

'Coffee would be better. I can't face any more alcohol.'

He remained in the living-room while she went to make it, and when she returned with it several moments later she was amused to see he was fast asleep. Setting down the cup on the table beside him, she moved closed to him. He had taken off his jacket, and his shirt clung to his skin, drawing her gaze to the muscles clearly visible beneath the material.

As if aware of being watched, he opened his eyes, then quickly sat up straight. 'Forgive me. I usually go out like a light when I fly, but this time I had a lot on my mind. You,' he explained, catching her hand and drawing her down to sit beside him.

'Why not have a proper sleep for an hour?' she suggested, annoyed with herself for still feeling nervous with him. 'You look as if you need it.'

'I need other things more,' he groaned, pulling her into his arms and caressing her breasts.

Lindsey willed herself to respond but failed. She was conscious of Robert's fingers gently sliding across her nipples, and though they hardened at his touch the only urge she felt was to push him away.

'Robert, don't.'

His arms dropped to his sides and his features grew hard. 'Is there someone else!'

'No. No one. It's what I said before. I'm scared.'

'Why? You're not a frightened virgin.'

'There's been . . .' She paused, moistening her lips. 'There's been no man since my—since my husband and I separated.'

He did not attempt to hide his astonishment, and as he absorbed what she had said, a furrow lined his brow. 'Is it because you're still in love with him, or are you afraid of being hurt again?'

'I'm not sure I can sustain a relationship,' she replied, not answering either question, and hoping he wouldn't notice.

'Don't give me that! You're an intelligent, subtle and caring woman who's simply scared of making another mistake.'

'OK, so I'm scared.'

'But you have to get over it. You can't live like a nun for the rest of your life.'

'I know. And when you walked in earlier, I thought I . . . but I can't.'

She forced herself to meet his eyes, seeing only compassion in them. She hadn't expected it, particularly when he had flown from one side of this vast country to the other for the very thing she was busy denying him!

'If you were legally free you'd find it easier to forget the past,' Robert stated. 'Get a divorce and marry me, Lindsey. We're right for each other.'

The unexpectedness of his proposal took her breath away. She knew he wanted her, but had never imagined he had marriage in mind.

'I wasn't anticipating this, Robert.'

'You can still give me an answer.'

'I can't. We barely know each other.'

'I know you're the woman I want as my wife. I'm not giving up on you, Lindsey. You were meant to be mine.'

She studied him, her head thrown back, her long white throat an alluring line. 'Part of your goods and chattels?'

'You should know me better than that. Our marriage will be a partnership. In fact I have excellent TV contacts that——'

'So have I,' she cut in. 'I've been offered my own show in England many times.'

'Then accept the offer and come home.'

'Has anyone ever likened you to a bulldozer?' she questioned drily.

'Many times. But it's got me where I am today, so I'm not about to change the way I behave. Anyway, it will help me get *you*,' he added confidently.

Lindsey remembered this as she paced the empty apartment after he had left. Robert's proposal had forced her to think of her future and what part he could play in it, but unfortunately Tim's image kept intruding. His silence these past four years spoke for itself, and she was crazy to go on harbouring the hope that they might get back together. She should close the door on the past and look forward.

But was it forward with Robert? As his wife, she would have the best of both worlds: her career, and a personal life as exciting and interesting. So what was holding her back? Why didn't she jump at his proposal?

It was an answer she had to find. Until she did, happiness would always elude her.

CHAPTER SEVEN

LINDSEY still hadn't made up her mind about Robert when she saw him off at Kennedy Airport, though she felt unusually lost as he hugged her close.

'I'm not letting you go now I've found you,' he warned her, his brown eyes gazing piercingly into her green ones.

'I won't hold you to that,' she teased. 'One should always discount what a man says when he's drunk or saying goodbye!'

'I'm one man you should never discount,' he stated. 'I want you to come to England and give yourself a chance with me. You can't go on living in limbo.'

'That's one thing you've made me realise.' She rested against him. How unpredictable she was! Now that he was leaving, the idea of his making love to her excited her. 'Robert, I——'

'You've no reason to remain here,' he cut in. 'Come back to England.'

'If I do, you'll see it as a commitment.'

'I promise I won't.' He released her. 'Look, you have almost four months free before you start work again, and you told me last night you don't know what to do with yourself, so why not come and work for me?'

'Work for *you*?' She was astonished. 'Doing what?'

'Helping me with my research on environmental pollution.'

'I never knew you were interested in that.'

'I have been for years. I put ten per cent of my company profits into it. And right now there's a mass of information that needs sorting out. Anthea—my assistant on the project—can't cope with it all.'

'Are you sure you aren't trying to create a job for me?'

'Certainly not. It's there, waiting for someone to take it. It will give you a chance to see what a tyrant I can be,' he joked. 'Think it over, Lindsey. It might even make a documentary for you—the way business people in different countries are tackling pollution. If we wait for governments to do something, our planet will be ruined before they get through the red tape.'

'That's true,' she agreed, amused by his ingenuity in turning his offer into one she could accept on a professional rather than an emotional level. 'I'll consider it.'

'Good.'

Then he was gone, pausing for an instant at the barrier to turn and wave before he disappeared.

Dejectedly she returned home, wishing she had allowed him to make love to her when she had had the chance. He was right about her not continuing to live in limbo. If she wasn't careful she'd become a dried-up shell. She had almost forgotten what it was like to go to bed with a man.

As if to seek reassurance, she peered at herself in the mirror. The luminescence of her skin owed more to Estee Lauder than to youth, though even devoid of make-up it was still fresh and unlined. Her green eyes shone clear and bright, and though a few extra pounds would not come amiss on her slender frame, her breasts were still full enough to turn the head of most red-blooded males.

But wasn't there an air of withdrawal about her? As if she had wrapped an invisible cloak around herself? She stepped back from the mirror in dismay. One way or another she had to rid herself of the past; and ending her marriage was the first step. After four years apart there should be no problem, and if Tim refused to do anything, *she* would.

That evening she wrote to tell him she wanted a divorce. Her letter was not unfriendly, and to her surprise she no longer felt any regret or bitterness. Robert had been her catharsis. There and then she determined to spend her vacation in England.

Everyone in the office noticed how much lighter her mood was, though Phil was the only one to guess the real reason she was going to London.

'It's Robert, isn't it?'

'Yes. He wants to marry me, but I'm not sure how I feel.'

'Don't rush into anything.' Phil's face creased into fatherly concern. 'I guess you'll be seeing your husband?'

'There's no point. I've written and asked him to arrange a divorce, and raking over the ashes is profitless.'

'If you decide not to come back, let me know as soon as you can. It won't be easy finding a replacement for you.'

'I'll bet,' Lindsey snorted. 'There must be thousands of girls out there dying for the chance!'

'Ten thousand, more likely, but *you're* one in a million—and you call tell Robert I said so.'

He called her that evening, and when she told him of her decision he was stunned into silence.

'You mean it?' he finally exploded. 'My God! That's great!'

'I'll be over in a month. I'm not sure how long I'll stay,' she added hurriedly, anxious to brake his enthusiasm. 'But that idea of yours for a documentary is worth exploring.'

'I'm glad you think so,' Robert said shakily. 'I'll see about finding you an apartment. It will be more convenient than a hotel.'

'No, please! I'll book into a hotel and look around for myself.'

'Why will it take you four weeks to get here?'

'Because I have to let my apartment and find a temporary home for Angus.'

'Bring him with you.'

'He'd have to be in quarantine for six months, and if I return to New York I'd have made him miserable for nothing.'

'Think how miserable you'd make *me* if you didn't stay!' Robert's voice deepened. 'I'll be counting the days till I see you.'

Lindsey found it easier to pick up her tracks than it had been to lay them, and within a week she had let her apartment and found a middle-aged couple eager to look after Angus.

A month after Robert's departure, she landed at Heathrow, where he was waiting to meet her. He gripped her hand but greeted her formally, which she found so unexpected that she gave him a surprised look.

'There's a photographer behind me, a few yards to the left, and if I so much as give you a peck on the cheek it will be in the national tabloids in the morning.'

'I'm very impressed,' she joked. 'I know you have a large company, but I hadn't realised you were so newsworthy.'

'Ordinarily I'm not. But at the moment I've a take-over battle on my hands, and in the last week it's hotted up. I'll tell you more in the car.'

In the back of his chauffeur-driven Jaguar, Robert sat close to her, his thigh pressing against hers. Inexplicably she felt nervous of him and only after they had chatted idly for several moments did she relax and again feel she had done the right thing in coming here.

'Incidentally, I've found you an apartment,' he announced as they neared London, 'so I cancelled your hotel booking.'

'But I said I'd look around when I got here.' She was irritated by his high-handedness, and Robert, aware of it, placed his hand over hers.

'Why waste money even for a few days? I knew this place was available and I was able to get it for you.'

Anxious not to spoil their first day together in England, Lindsey capitulated. 'Where is it?' she asked.

'In Knightsbridge.'

She gave an involuntary start, his words reviving memories of Patsy, but luckily he didn't notice and went on talking.

'It's in a small modern block belonging to a friend of mine. That's how I managed to get it.'

His obvious pleasure at having done something for her would have made further protest churlish, and she said no more.

'It also has the advantage of not being too far from my office,' he went on a few moments later as they entered the small but expensively furnished apartment in a beautiful, tree-lined square.

'It's lovely,' she murmured, looking around.

'I'm glad you like it.' He came to stand beside her. 'I think you'll enjoy being in my office too. Anthea can't wait to meet you. She was in the States for Christmas and saw you in one of your documentaries, so you have a ready-made fan!' Lightly he touched her cheek. 'I'll leave you to unpack and have a rest. I have a late meeting scheduled for tonight, but I'd like to have dinner with you first, if that's all right with you?'

'Of course it is.'

He came a step closer to her, his full lower lip jutting forward. 'You *have* returned because of me, haven't you, Lindsey?'

'You certainly precipitated it,' she admitted. 'But it was time I came back. I've written and told my husband I'd like a divorce, and if he still doesn't do anything about it, it will be easier for me to instruct a lawyer if I'm here. That doesn't mean I'm ready to get married again,' she said hastily as she saw his face brighten. 'I'm not making any promises, Robert.'

'Fair enough, but am I allowed to hope?'

'I can't stop you,' she smiled.

'And may I cherish you from time to time—like sending my chauffeur to collect you this evening?'

'Absolutely. Every girl needs an occasional cherish!'

Happy with her answer, he left and, closing the door behind him, Lindsey could not restrain a sigh. It was not in his nature to be patient. He was the type to charge full steam ahead to achieve his goals, but she had no intention of being a pushover and, if necessary, he would have to learn it the hard way.

She spent the rest of the day unpacking and settling into the apartment. She shopped for basic foods, wandered round a couple of department stores and returned home to rest for a few hours.

Refreshed, she showered and dressed for her date with Robert, feeling a pleasurable sense of excitement as she stepped into the chauffeur-driven car that came to collect her at seven-thirty.

She was in no way surprised when she was deposited at a private dining club off Park Lane, and as she entered the oak-panelled lobby Robert came forward to greet her.

In a navy suit and white shirt that exaggerated his dark hair and tanned skin, he oozed confidence and charm. 'Now I really believe you're in England,' he exclaimed, taking her elbow.

'I'm finally realising it myself,' she confessed. 'I feel as if I have been away years. The streets are narrower, the buildings smaller. Everything's changed.'

'Perhaps it's *you* who have changed.'

'That too. It wasn't until I set foot in England again that I became aware of it.' She slanted him a smile. 'I'm not sure you would have liked the old me.'

He did not question this until they were seated at their table. 'What wouldn't I have liked about the old you?'

'I wouldn't dream of telling you! It might turn you against me!'

'Nothing could do that. I'm crazy about you.'

'Don't say that,' she said swiftly.

'Why not?'

'I don't want you to be hurt. And if you read too much into my coming to England...'

'I promise not to read anything into it. Satisfied?'

'Yes,' she said, but didn't mean it, knowing full well that Robert hadn't meant what he had said either.

'I'm sorry I have to leave you after dinner,' he apologised. 'But I'm meeting Ramsden. He's the new boss of the Semperton Trust.'

Lindsey's heart seemed to leap into her throat. 'I—I know.' She marvelled that her voice sounded so calm. 'I read about him recently in *Time* magazine.'

'Haven't we all!'

'You don't like him?' She was quick to pick up on Robert's tone.

'Let's say I'd like him more if he were running another company. But he's got his sights on an engineering firm that *I'm* determined to buy. That's why I'm meeting him. To try to persuade him to back down.'

'He may be seeing you for the same reason!'

'I'm sure he is. You know what these upper-crust types are like. Think they run the world and everyone will do their bidding.' Robert's jaw clenched. 'Not that he's aggressive in manner. On the contrary; he's quiet, polite, charming.'

This was a good description of her father-in-law, Lindsey thought, and was about to confess his relationship to her when Robert banged his hand on the table.

'But all the more dangerous because of it,' he exclaimed.

'Dangerous?'

'You forget to keep up your guard. And the moment you lower it, he goes in for the kill.'

Lindsey gave Robert a warm smile. 'I'd back you against Mr Ramsden any day.'

'Thanks for the vote of confidence.'

'I mean it,' she reiterated. 'You've already achieved so much.'

'I'll admit that the day you marry me.'

She shook her head at him and he grinned at her, totally unabashed.

During their meal she was conscious of many eyes watching them, and for the first time appreciated what it was like to go out with a man who was well known. It made her question whether it was wise for her to work for him when it was quite on the cards that he and her father-in-law might become engaged in some business battle. Yet why should she let any of the Ramsdens affect her life? She was a free agent and could do as she pleased. Setting down her glass, she gave Robert a wide smile, and he responded by pressing her hand under the table.

'I wish I wasn't tied up tonight,' he grumbled. 'But it's only two days to the weekend. You *will* spend it with me, won't you? I promised you no strings, and I'll stand by that.'

'Thank you.'

'You sound like a little girl when you say that.'

She smiled, but deep inside her knew it was an indictment of her present emotional state. Or perhaps it was truer to call it a lack of an emotional state. For that was what came of putting one's feelings into storage: they atrophied. Damn it, she shouldn't be wanting a platonic relationship with this handsome, intelligent man who so obviously wanted more from her. She should be eager for his touch, yearning for his closeness. Instead of which she was still hankering for——

Stop it! she ordered herself. For the sake of your sanity, stop it.

With a start she saw that Robert was rising, and hastily she followed.

'It's only nine o'clock,' he said. 'If you aren't tired, why not drop in to see Anthea for a little while? My office is only a few minutes from here, and she's working late tonight. Then Murphy will drive you home.'

'I'd like that. It's always nice to meet one of my fans!' And even nicer, Lindsey thought, not to go back to a strange apartment and be alone with memories she didn't want to face. 'What does your assistant know about us?'

'That we're friends. Anthea's a no-nonsense young woman, and is completely loyal to me so you've nothing to worry about.'

They climbed into the back of the Jaguar and it glided away from the kerb. Robert reached for Lindsey's hand, clasping it close and drawing it down to his thigh.

With an effort, she managed to keep it relaxed, and hoped he wasn't aware how fast her pulse was racing.

'It's fantastic having you here with me,' he murmured softly, caressing her fingers. 'When you're close to me, I feel I can conquer the world.'

Lindsey kept her voice light. 'Keep that thought with you when you're with Mr Ramsden!'

Robert chuckled. 'I'll do that. It's a great suggestion.'

The car slowed down and stopped outside a modern office block and he got out ahead of her and escorted her to the entrance.

'Anthea's office is on the tenth floor. I'd take you up and introduce you, but I'm pressed for time.'

'Don't worry about it. I can introduce myself.'

'I'll send the car back for you.'

'That isn't necessary. I'll take a taxi.' Lindsey gave him a slight push. 'Go to your meeting and stop worrying about me.'

Squeezing her hand, he left her, and she made her way up to the tenth floor, where she was greeted by a plump, brown-haired woman in her early thirties, who was waiting for her as the lift door opened.

'I couldn't believe it when I heard you were joining us for a few months,' Anthea Connall beamed at her as she led her down a grey-carpeted corridor to a large, well-appointed suite of offices.

'I hope I can be of help,' Lindsay smiled back. 'I began my career as a researcher, so I'm not quite a novice.'

'I'm sure you aren't,' came the ardent reply.

'What hours do you work?'

'Mine are pretty elastic.' Anthea glanced down at her ringless hands. 'My boyfriend's very accommodating—unfortunately. But Mr Lawson said you should do whatever hours you like. He wants you to feel completely free.'

Lindsey doubted whether this would apply if she were married to him. Despite his assertion that as his wife she could do her own thing, she was sure he would always expect her to be available when he wanted her.

His wife. The thought gave her neither joy or anxiety. She felt absolutely nothing.

I'm not ready to make a commitment, she admitted to herself, and faced the unpalatable knowledge that returning to England had made her memories of Tim more vivid, making her wonder if she would ever be able to accept another man in her life.

CHAPTER EIGHT

ANY doubts Lindsey felt about working for Robert were dispelled by the third day. She had been convinced he had deliberately found work for her to do, but she now realised Anthea was swamped and probably needed not one but two assistants.

Her only disquiet was that Tim had not responded to the letter she had sent to him prior to leaving New York, and, anxious to straighten out her marital status without his knowing she was in London, she engaged Ellen Baxted, a lawyer Phil Marsham had suggested, to find out what was going on.

'Why not call him yourself?' the woman advised. 'It's preferable to leave lawyers out of it.'

'*You* say that?'

'I'm in the best position to do so!'

Lindsey smiled. 'I appreciate your honesty, but I don't want my husband to know I'm in England.'

'I see. In that case I'll write to him, and let you know when I have some news.'

Early Friday afternoon Lindsey left with Robert to spend the weekend at his country home. She had been surprised to learn it was a few miles outside Birmingham—having expected him to choose the Cotswolds or Sussex—and he had quickly picked up her thoughts.

'It's fifteen minutes' drive from my factory,' he explained. 'I try to spend three days a week there. I'm not the sort of boss who can leave things to others.'

'I can believe that!'

He chuckled. 'You know me too well. I wish I could say the same about *you*.'

She smiled and said nothing, but couldn't help wondering if she had been foolhardy in agreeing to stay with him. Well, she'd find out soon enough!

They reached his house—large and Georgian—in time for tea on the lawn. It was very much the 'property of a country gentleman', and she couldn't help wondering if he had dreamed of owning a such a house when, as a twelve-year-old, he had helped his widowed mother eke out the family income by mowing lawns and delivering newspapers.

'Your family must be proud of your success?' she commented.

'There was only my mother, and she said she always knew I'd make it to the top.' His face clouded. 'She died last year, and I think that's when I realised a career only fulfilled part of my life.' He reached for Lindsey's hand. 'You can fill the rest of it for me.'

'That's a lovely compliment,' she said huskily. 'But you're being too flattering.'

To her relief he did not pursue the subject and, tea finished, he suggested they went for a walk.

'A city-type walk or a real country one?' she questioned.

'A real one,' he replied, and was as good as his word, tramping steadily for mile after mile until they reached a delightful inn, where they dined simply, but well, before ordering a cab to take them home.

Lindsey could not restrain a yawn as they entered the lamplit hall, just after ten o'clock. 'Sorry. It's all the air and exercise.'

'As long as it isn't my company!'

She grinned, and he put his hand under her elbow and guided her upstairs.

Her bedroom was at the opposite end of the corridor from his, a gesture she appreciated, as she did the chaste kiss he gave her when he left her at the door.

She lay sleepless for a long time, enjoying the silk sheet beneath her and the goosedown duvet above her. The house was perfect in every way: furnished with an understated elegance that cost a fortune, and presided over with quiet efficiency by a Spanish couple. There would be no hardship in becoming the châtelaine here, she thought. All she had to do was say yes. But could she?

She was asleep before she found the answer.

Saturday they explored the antiques shops in the nearby town, and in the evening saw a new play being tried out in the local theatre.

Sunday was rain-filled, and they spent the morning reading the papers, and the afternoon in the barn alongside the house, which had been turned into a vast games-room, complete with heated swimming-pool.

'Not bad for a working class millionaire?' he joked.

'Not bad for a caring member of society,' she countered, and was touched to see him redden.

He beat her soundly at table tennis, after which they cooled off in the water. Undressed, he was hirsute and muscular, and it was easy to see him as a caveman, flinging his woman over his shoulder and carrying her back to his lair.

Lindsey couldn't restrain the shiver of desire that coursed through her body, and hastily dived below the water, emerging several yards beyond him, a distance she maintained until he heaved himself out and settled in a lounger, watching her as she ploughed tirelessly backwards and forwards.

'I knew you'd be an excellent swimmer as soon as I saw your costume,' he teased. 'Only a real swimmer would wear such a creation!'

Laughing, she glanced down at her serviceable black one-piece. 'Were you anticipating a bikini?'

'I can dream, can't I?' He reached for her, then quickly dropped his hands.

The gesture—of fear that he was annoying her, showed how desperately he was trying to conform to her wishes. What right do I have to minimise him like this? she chas-

tised herself. If I can't see my future with him, I should
never have agreed to work for him. What a bitch I am!

Without thinking, she took a step towards him, and
his arms instantly clasped her close. He was warm and
dry, and with a gasp of apology she tried to draw back,
but he wouldn't let her.

'No, don't move. This is where you belong. I love you,
Lindsey; when are you going to drop the barriers and
start living again?'

'Give me time,' she pleaded, and tilting her head,
kissed him tenderly, sorry for the pain she was causing
him.

With a ferocity that took her by surprise, his lips forced
hers apart, his tongue probing deep as his hands cupped
her buttocks and pressed her firmly against his arousal.

Determinedly she tried to respond, knowing this was
her best hope of forgetting Tim, of finally slaying the
dragon that had bedevilled her for almost five years.
Unresisting, she let him draw her down upon the lounger.

'You're perfect,' he groaned as his hands roughly
roamed her body and, as she tensed, he pulled down the
top of her swimsuit and took her nipple in his mouth.

His teeth nipped rather than teased, and his touch was
almost brutal as his fingers dug too deep, hurting instead of arousing. Yet having instigated their lovemaking, guilt forced Lindsey to feign a passion she was
far from feeling, for all she could think of was Tim, and
she finally admitted that there could be no one else for
her; that he was the only man she wanted and would
ever love.

Tim, she cried silently again, and though Robert
couldn't hear it, the tears coursing down her cheeks wet
his face, and he interpreted it as a sign of passion and
pressed his body heavily upon hers, his knee forcing her
legs apart.

'I'm crazy about you,' he said thickly, and began
pulling down his swimming trunks.

Mortified that she had put herself in this embarrassing situation, she searched for a way out that wouldn't humiliate him, and suddenly became aware of the screech of tyres on gravel, followed by the slam of a car door.

'Someone's arrived!' she whispered urgently, feeling like a prize fighter saved by the bell.

Voices sounded close by, a man and a woman, and Robert jack-knifed up and reached for his towelling robe.

'It's Bert Elkins, my public relations advisor, and his wife,' he muttered angrily. 'The times I've asked him not to come here without calling me first!' He strode to the door. 'Coming, Lindsey?'

'Not for the moment. I'll join you later.'

Only when she was in the safety of her bedroom did she once again let herself think of Robert's lovemaking. Was it because she was still legally tied to Tim that she had reacted against it so violently? And if so, would she feel differently once she was free? Even as the question arose, she remembered the roughness of Robert's touch, and shuddered.

But was she being fair to him? If she had genuinely responded to him perhaps he'd have been gentler, but he could well have sensed her lack of passion and been trying to arouse her.

So where did it leave her now, and what in heaven's name should she do? Only one thing was certain. Until she had her divorce and could regard herself as single again, she had to keep him at arm's length.

As things turned out, this wasn't as much of a problem as she had feared. Bert Elkins and his wife stayed to dinner, and shortly after they left she and Robert drove back to London.

He was out of town most of the following week, during which she saw several old friends, and also had lunch with Grace Chapman, now programme controller of Universal TV who made no bones about wanting her to stay in London permanently and front her own series.

Saying she would be delighted to accept the offer if she remained in England, Lindsey returned to the office.

As she walked in, there was a call from Robert.

'I'm at home, packing,' he stated abruptly. 'I have to go to Milan.'

'For how long?'

'Four or five days. I'm sorry about this. I'll miss you.'

Uncomfortably aware that he might be expecting her to echo this sentiment, she said hurriedly, 'You sound a bit agitated.'

'Furious is a better word. I heard this morning that Semperton Trust may be bidding for Malvini, the Italian company I'm trying to buy. Ramsden, blast him, seems determined to buy up every engineering company he can.'

'Including yours?' Lindsey joked.

'That's a distinct possibility.' There was no humour in Robert's answer. 'That's why I want to buy Malvini. If I succeed, it wouldn't be so easy for Ramsden to swallow me.'

Lindsey wondered what Robert would say if she told him her husband was the son of the man he had just castigated. Sooner or later he had to know, but it was hardly the sort of news to spring on him over the telephone. Far better to choose a more appropriate time.

'Think of me while I'm gone,' he murmured. 'And remember that I love you and I'm a patient man.'

To her surprise, Lindsey did remember this, and during the weekend thought of him with unusual warmth. Was it because she knew she would shortly be single and was feeling unexpectedly vulnerable? After all, what price success when one returned to an empty apartment at night? When there was no special loved one to share the highs and lows? But was Robert the right man with whom to share them?

Sadly, the answer still eluded her.

CHAPTER NINE

ON MONDAY morning, recollecting a psychologist friend in New York saying that the more uncertain you felt, the more positive you should try to look, Lindsey donned one of her favourite outfits—an Escada suit in emerald-green linen that turned her hair to flame and her slenderness to sexiness.

'Wow!' Anthea greeted her as she entered the office. 'Anything special on your agenda today?'

'No. Anything on yours?'

'Not unless you regard a trip to Liverpool as a rave-up!' Anthea was on the threshold when she paused. 'Oh, I nearly forgot. Mr Ramsden's stopping by for a folder—the pink one on my desk.'

Lindsey couldn't believe she had heard correctly. 'Mr Ramsden is coming *here*?'

'Amazing, isn't it, when you think how Mr Lawson hates his guts! But that's big business for you. It seems that when they had their meeting the other evening, Mr Ramsden was interested in getting a quotation from us to do some work for them.'

'But Semperton has its own engineering company,' Lindsey exclaimed.

'Apparently they aren't geared up to do this particular job. Anyway, Mr Ramsden's secretary rang and said he was seeing someone in the building next door and would call in on his way there.'

'C-can't I send it across to him?'

'No, he'll be here any minute.'

The door closed behind her and Lindsey reached for the file with shaking hands. Would Mr Ramsden recognise her after nearly five years, considering how infrequently they had met? And what would he say if he did?

Lost in thought, she was brought back to the present by an incisive rap on the door, and stiffening her shoulders she called, 'Come in.'

The man who did was a younger, wide-shouldered, vibrant version of her father-in-law, and her heart hammered in her breast as she stared at him.

'Tim!' Her throat tightened with shock and she was unable to say another word.

Not so Tim. Despite his obvious surprise, he advanced into the room with confident strides and equally confident voice. 'This is very unexpected, Lindsey. I thought you were in the States.'

His voice had changed to match his assured manner, and though it had the faint drawl she remembered, there was now an incisive edge to it.

'I've been back several weeks,' she replied.

His eyes flicked round the room. 'What are you doing *here*?'

'I work for Robert Lawson.'

'You *what*?'

It was a blatant show of displeasure. Hardly surprising in view of what Robert had told her.

'It's damned awkward,' he stated, confirming her thoughts.

Lindsey remained silent. Awkward or not, Tim and his father could lump it.

'Extremely awkward,' he repeated, slipping one hand into the pocket of his jacket, a movement that was familiar yet different.

The Tim of old, when angry, had bunched both hands in his pockets, quickly causing his jackets to lose shape. But now he just did it with the fingers of one hand, the sign becoming more subtle, and not disturbing the faultless cut of his suit. Nor was he as thin as he used to be; the hollows beneath his cheeks had filled out, adding firmness to features that were still as chiselled as if carved from stone. Even his hair was different; worn shorter, it appeared blonder and thicker. How she had loved to run her fingers through its silkiness, to feel it against her breasts as his lips had suckled her...

Abruptly she held out the pink file. 'This is for your father.'

'My father?'

'It's the estimate he wanted. I assume you've come to collect it for him.'

The corners of Tim's mouth curled slightly upwards. Hardly strong enough to be called a smile, it held more the suggestion of irony. 'You're half right, at least. I *have* come for the file, but it's for me. My father retired years ago; soon after——' the hesitation was slight '—soon after you went to the States.'

It was the second shock Lindsey had received in a matter of minutes, but a far more difficult one to swallow.

'Do you—you mean *you* are the Mr Ramsden that Semperton Trust wanted to get their hands on? Not your father?'

'Not my father,' Tim confirmed, his tone dry as dust. 'Let's say I joined the family firm at the right time. Or, as you would doubtless put it, I was there by hereditary right!'

Lindsey didn't blame him for his sarcasm, for the girl she had once been would certainly have said it. But today there was one thing she knew for sure: if the Semperton board had wanted him, it was because of his ability, not his birthright. But to say so to Tim was tantamount to admitting that many of her views had changed, and this could raise a host of other questions from him. Questions she would be loath to answer in view of the fact that over the years he had never attempted to get in touch with her.

'I—I had no idea you were so successful,' she murmured, and as her eyes met his cool, watchful grey ones, and saw no desire flaring in them, she felt the chill of desolation seep into her soul.

'Why should you have known, given our lack of communication these past five years?' he answered flatly.

'I wrote to you twice,' she reminded him.

'Once to confirm you were going to New York for six months, and the second time to say you were remaining there for the foreseeable future.'

'You could still have written.'

'What was there to say? You left *me*, not the other way around, remember?'

'How could I forget?' she replied trenchantly. 'How *is* Patsy, by the way?'

'Fine.'

His casual tone infuriated her, and despite longing to know what their relationship was she would die before giving him the satisfaction of knowing she cared enough to ask. And she did care. The swelling of her breasts as she eyed him, the lurch in her stomach as he had come towards her, had confirmed it.

It's nothing other than desire, she chided herself. It has nothing to do with love. Tim's even handsomer now than he was years ago, and I'm a sexually frustrated young woman. So why shouldn't I fancy him? But it isn't love and it will disappear once I'm free to give myself to Robert. Satisfied by her logic, she leaned back in her chair.

'Now you're here, we should discuss our divorce. If you won't file for it, I will.'

'I'd rather you didn't for the moment,' he informed her quietly.

Was this his way of telling her he wished to have her back? A surge of hope, strong as a spring tide, swept over her. 'Why?' she asked huskily.

'Don't play the innocent with me,' he stated. 'Working for Lawson, you're surely aware of the reason?'

Hope died and anger sparked through her. 'As a matter of fact I've no idea what you're talking about, and if you can't be civil, I suggest you let your lawyer do the talking.'

'Sorry—that was rude of me.'

The Tim of old would have made some bodily movement of embarrassment and looked away. But today he met her eyes and maintained his stance. Here was no callow young man ready to yield to her every whim, but a person answerable only to himself.

'As you're working for Lawson,' he went on, 'I automatically presumed you'd know what I meant.'

'Well, I don't. So if you'd care to enlighten me...'

'Semperton's may soon be engaged in a takeover battle for Malvini,' Tim stated in even tones, 'and since I'm the chairman and very involved in the matter, the newspapers would have a great time writing up my divorce.'

'What could they say about it? We've been separated long enough to get one, so it won't be necessary for me to cite any other woman.'

Tim stared at her, and she had the impression he wanted to say more but was debating whether he should. 'We've waited almost five years,' he said finally. 'Surely you can wait a little longer—or are you in a hurry to remarry?'

Lindsey hesitated, then decided to be honest. 'Robert Lawson has asked me.'

'I see.'

Tim sounded so unmoved that she had an urge to knock his ego. 'We met in New York a couple of months ago, and hit it off immediately. That's why I decided to spend the summer here. The second time around I want to be sure I'm not making a mistake,' she added for good measure, aware that every word was bringing her nearer to accepting Robert's proposal. Yet she felt no panic. Maybe it had needed the sight of Tim to help her decide.

'I'm glad you've finally found someone you can love.' There was no sarcasm in his voice. 'I wish you every happiness.'

'Thank you.'

'But I still hope you'll consider doing as I've asked.'

'To help your career?' she questioned. 'I'd have thought you were already at the top. From what I've heard about your record at Semperton Trust, you're an excellent chairman. Not great as a husband, of course,' she couldn't resist adding, anxious to show she cared so little about the past that she could joke about it.

'I hope *I'll* do better the second time around too,' he replied. 'But for the moment I'd prefer to stay married to *you*.'

'Don't push me, Tim. Robert will be back in a few days and I'll discuss it with him. If he's prepared to wait, I'll do as you ask.'

'I'm sure you haven't lost the art of persuasion.'

A blush stained her cheeks, intensifying as Tim leaned down towards her. But it was merely to take the pink folder she was holding, and she caught her breath, feeling incredibly foolish.

'I'll be seeing you,' he said, and sauntered out.

How controlled he was. Far more today than when they had first married, which made it harder for her to read him. But at least she now knew why he had been content to let their marriage continue: not because he had hoped for a reconciliation, but because legally ending it had not suited him politically.

Didn't Patsy mind or weren't they together? And what about his parents? They would certainly want him to have a son and heir, which he wouldn't have until he remarried. Still, he was only thirty-two, remarkably young to be in charge of such a vast company, and young enough to wait several years before starting a family.

The thought of Tim with children was an image she didn't care to think about, and she pushed it aside. She had told him that whether she did as he asked depended on Robert, but she had been lying. She would make the decision, and no one else, but as of now, she had no idea which way to jump.

'Quit lying to yourself!' she muttered aloud. 'You don't want to harm Tim's career, and if staying married to him for few months will help him, you'll do it.'

But how to tell Robert without his thinking she was still in love with Tim? And that wasn't all she had to tell him. She must also confess that his business rival was the very one she was trying to help!

'Timothy Ramsden, your *husband*?' Robert echoed her statement, his voice astounded. 'Why in hell didn't you tell me before?'

'When you spoke of him, I assumed it was my father-in-law.'

'You should still have told me you were related to him. Why keep it a secret?'

'I felt you didn't like me talking about my marriage. You never referred to it.'

'Because it seemed a touchy subject and I didn't want to upset you.'

'It wouldn't have upset me,' Lindsey retorted. 'Tim means nothing to me.'

'Then why are you considering doing as he wants?'

Realising that to tell him the truth would disclose how muddled her feelings were for Tim, she sought for the next most logical reason.

'He isn't my enemy, and if divorcing him now could harm him, it's spiteful to refuse.'

Robert opened his mouth to speak, then closed it without saying anything, reminding Lindsey that Tim had behaved in a similar fashion a couple of days ago.

'Anyway, I'll only be delaying the divorce for a couple of months,' she added.

'Put like that, it would be churlish of me to try to argue you out of it.'

Pleased that Robert had agreed without giving her too much hassle, Lindsey relaxed. He had called her from Milan to say he was arriving at Heathrow at seven and, anxious to unburden herself, she had invited him to dinner, waiting till they reached the coffee stage before confessing her husband's identity and the request he had made to her two days ago.

'There's only one thing I'd like to say,' Robert vouchsafed into the silence. 'I hope you won't forget that you came to England to spend time with me.'

'I'll be seeing you in the office each day,' she promised, 'and we'll have to be discreet about being seen together outside.'

'That suits *me*,' he chuckled. 'We can meet at your place or mine!'

Warning bells rang in Lindsey's head, but she gave no visible sign of it, though after he had gone she tried to envisage herself as his wife. But as always the memory of her marriage to Tim overshadowed it. Yet if truth were told, her marriage had never been totally happy, for she had always been afraid that one day pressure from his family would induce Tim to leave her.

His family. Even now she couldn't think of her mother-in-law without bitterness, remembering the slights, the snobbishness, the lack of warmth. But why waste time rehashing the past? She was a different person today: confident of herself, mature enough to be her own woman and make her own decisions. Refusing to help Tim was a good way of thumbing her nose at his mother, but it would also make her as mean spirited as Mrs Ramsden had been.

Not surprisingly, when she finally fell asleep it was to dream of Tim making love to her, and she awakened aching for him, her breasts swollen with desire.

I'm out of my head, she told herself furiously. Robert is far more suitable for me, and the sooner I accept that the better.

'You're suffering from four a.m. blues,' she stated aloud, and hearing her voice, vibrant and angry, came back fast to the reality of today; of today with Robert, and tomorrow with Robert too. All her tomorrows, and Tim wouldn't figure in any of them. Oh, yes, she'd help him; not because she loved him but because she didn't want it on her conscience that she had done anything to jeopardise his career. That was one guilt she could do without!

At eight in the morning she dialled Tim's number and he picked up the receiver at the first ring. 'I'll do as you asked,' she announced without preamble.

'Thank you. I wasn't sure you would.'

'I'm not your enemy, Tim: and Robert has agreed to wait, so it's no problem for me.'

'I'm glad,' came the cool response. 'Thanks again.'

'Don't mention it.'

Despite the calmness of her voice, Lindsey's hands were shaking as she replaced the telephone, reminding her that what one said often bore no relationship to how one felt.

Ten o'clock found her in Robert's office, and she was transferring some notes on to her word processor when a small, wiry man came in. He had a weatherbeaten face crisscrossed with fine lines, and spiky eyebrows that matched his grey, shaggy hair. His dishevelled look did nothing to suggest he was one of Robert's associates, yet instinctively she knew he was not an ordinary member of the public.

'I'm Jack Dunford, Mrs Ramsden,' he abruptly introduced himself. 'I'm personal assistant to your husband, and I'd like to talk to you.'

Lindsey drew a sharp breath. It was years since anyone had called her by her married name, and as if aware of her discomfiture the man half smiled.

'May we go somewhere quiet where we won't be disturbed?' he went on.

'We'll be fine here,' she assured him, and waited while he pulled forward a chair and sat down.

'I gather you have agreed to delay your divorce,' the man said. 'But I have another favour to ask of you.'

'Did Tim send you?'

'You must be kidding! He'd have my hide if he knew I was here.'

'Then perhaps you should go.'

'Not until I have said my piece.' Dunford's jaw squared pugnaciously. 'I want you to stop working for Mr Lawson.'

'Why?'

'Come, come, Mrs Ramsden, you know the answer to that as well as I do. He'll be fighting your husband for control of Malvini, and if the newshounds discovered you were working for him they'd have a field day.'

'Why should they?'

'For one thing it would look as if you took this job to discredit Tim—side with his opponent, so to speak.'

'That's absurd.'

'*I* know that, and so does Tim, but how would it look from an outside viewpoint?' Jack Dunford laid his hands on her desk, and Lindsey noticed the nails were short and blunt, in keeping with his character. 'That's why I want you to quit working here. When our takeover bid for Malvini has succeeded, you can——'

'Mr Lawson may win!'

'Let's not argue over that one. Just do as I ask. If you're not Tim's enemy——'

'Damn it, Mr Dunford, if I *were*, I wouldn't have agreed to——'

'OK, OK, I apologise for that. But just stop working *here*.'

'I'm not sure I can. Mr Lawson might be very upset.'

'I doubt it. In fact I'm amazed he hasn't asked you himself to quit.'

Lindsey frowned. 'Why do I feel that there's something I should have worked out but haven't?' She eyed the pugnacious little man in front of her. 'Will *you* tell me exactly what's going on?'

'Only if Lawson doesn't. But ask him first.' Jack Dunford went to the door. 'Will you do that?'

'You're expecting a lot, Mr Dunford.'

'I don't think I am. I'm a great admirer of your husband, Mrs Ramsden. He's brilliant, and honest with it. An all too rare combination in the business world these days, and he deserves to win.'

'No comment,' Lindsey said drily. 'My loyalties are with Mr Lawson.'

'Yes, well...' Jack Dunford stopped short. 'I'll be seeing you.'

The door closed behind him, but the questions he had raised and the request he had made remained to trouble her. Something was strange about this Malvini affair, and she was determined to make Robert tell her what it was. Hell's bells, she wasn't an investigative film maker for nothing!

CHAPTER TEN

EVEN before she had spoken to Robert, Lindsey resolved to stop working for him. Honesty made her admit she was doing it as much for herself as for Tim, for until she had reached a conclusion about a future with Robert it was kinder not to give him too much hope.

Unexpectedly he took her that evening to a party given by some close friends of his. It was the first time he had introduced her into his social circle, and she couldn't help comparing it with Tim's, which had consisted of the county set and amateur sports people. Of course the milieu he mixed in today had probably changed, but she couldn't see it being quite the newly rich, upwardly mobile one favoured by Robert.

She told no one she was working for him, and when cornered by a famous financial journalist kept a tight rein on her tongue.

'I wish you'd warned me where we were going tonight,' she commented as Robert drove her home. 'It was pure luck I was suitably dressed.'

'You always are, my darling. The only reason I didn't tell you was that I didn't want you getting uptight at the prospect of meeting my friends.' His voice deepened. 'I wish I could have introduced you as my future wife.'

Here was the opportunity to say she couldn't continue working for him, but as she went to do so they drew up outside her apartment block and, anxious to clear the air while she still had the courage, she invited him in for a nightcap.

She went directly to the drinks tray as he shut the front door behind him. 'Whisky or brandy?'

'Brandy,' he answered easily, and stood beside her while she poured.

'How did your trip to Milan go?' she asked lightly as she handed him his glass. 'You never did tell me.'

'It went pretty much as I expected.' The look he gave her was keen. 'What did Ramsden tell you about it?'

'Why should I have asked *him*? You were the one who went.' Anger trembled through her but she did not allow it to show in her voice. 'But as you seem suspicious of my motive, it's probably best if I stop working for you. Then you won't feel you have a spy on the premises.'

'Don't be ridiculous! Look, I'm sorry I was sharp-tongued, but I was given the run-around in Milan and then to come back and learn that your husband is one of my biggest business rivals...' He stopped abruptly, thick eyebrows drawn together in concentration. 'This thing with Malvini... Ramsden is definitely going to put in a bid for the company, so it's partly a question of who's prepared to pay the most.'

'Partly.' Intelligence sharp, she picked up on the word. 'What do you mean by partly? What else, apart from money, can swing the bid?'

'Not what, but who. Carlo Malvini himself. He's the biggest shareholder. He also happens to be a devoutly religious man who believes in the sanctity of marriage. Hence Ramsden asking you to hold off on your divorce. My bet is that he's already told him how happily married he is. Heck! If I'd known about your relationship with Ramsden while I was in Milan, I'd have put Malvini wise.'

Lindsey's breath caught in her throat and Robert, hearing the sound, gave a second thought to what he had said and looked discomfited.

'No, I wouldn't,' he amended. 'That was temper talking, not common sense. And common sense would have made me keep quiet. After all, I'm caught up in the mess too. Here I am telling Malvini I regard marriage as a lifelong commitment, when in reality I can't wait to marry a woman who's in the act of getting rid of her husband!'

'That's a reality we can easily change,' Lindsey informed him. 'I haven't agreed to be your wife, you know. I've already warned you I'm still not sure of my feelings.'

'I'm sure enough for both of us!' Robert set down his glass. 'I love you, Lindsey, and I'd marry you if you had a dozen divorces behind you!'

'But not while the Malvini bid is still going on,' she stated, seeing by the flush that stained his face that he could not deny her comment.

'Can you blame me?' he asked.

She shook her head. 'All's fair in love and business! So, as I'm delaying the divorce not to tarnish Tim's golden boy image, it's only fair that I don't tarnish your image either. I'm going back to the States.'

'No!' It was a short, explosive sound, followed by Robert pulling her hard into his arms. 'Gaining control of Malvini is very important to me, for reasons you already know, but if it's a question of you or my business I'll choose *you* every time.'

'That's emotion talking, Robert. But I'm glad you said it.'

'I mean it.'

'And I mean it when I say I'm returning to the States.'

'That isn't necessary. We can still see each other discreetly. Then by the time the bid is out of the way you'll have had a chance to decide if you'll make me the happiest man in the world.'

Lindsey hesitated, then nodded. 'Very well.'

Long after Robert had left, she paced the floor, racked by questions that refused to go away. If she cared for him enough to consider marrying him, why was it taking her so long to make up her mind? Was it because she was scared of a second failure?

An image of Patsy rose before her. If the girl were still in Tim's life, surely she'd have pressed him for marriage? Not that the Tim of today could be coerced into doing anything he didn't want to do. Cool of face, cold of voice, he was no longer the warm, impulsive man she had known. Lindsey frowned. Had she changed as much as he had? Did he find *her* a stranger too? And if so, did he like or dislike what she had become?

The questions continued plaguing her long after she was in bed, and finding it impossible to sleep, she switched on the bedside lamp and reached for a book; safer to give herself over to someone else's thoughts than to allow her own free rein.

Next morning, she went to Robert's office early to clear her desk. Anthea arrived as she was finishing, and though taken aback to learn she was leaving, readily accepted her excuse that she had another television documentary to prepare.

As she left the building, she wondered whether to tell Jack Dunford she had done as he had asked or let him discover it for himself. She was reluctant to go to his office in case she bumped into Tim, but as the admission surfaced she gave an irritable shake of her head. She had no reason to be afraid. She had survived their last meeting and would survive another.

To her chagrin, she had no idea where Semperton Trust was housed. It was a huge conglomerate and each company might well be in different buildings. Indeed Tim's office, where Mr Dunford was to be found, might not even be listed in the directory. Heading for a telephone booth, she dialled Directory Enquiries and was told there was only one number and address for Semperton Trust.

Jotting it down, she hailed a taxi, and fifteen minutes later stood outside a steel and glass structure that towered into the blue sky above the River Thames. It wasn't what she had expected. But then, had she thought Tim would be working in a Regency house crammed with antiques? Shaking aside the fanciful thought—this aggressively modern structure was far more suited to the Tim of today—she stepped into the air-conditioned building and made for the marble-fronted reception counter.

'I'd like to see Mr Dunford,' she said, giving her name to one of the well spoken middle-aged women there.

'Do you have an appointment?'

'No. But if he's in, I'm sure he'll see me.'

Bestowing a dubious look on her, the woman dialled an extension, and ten seconds later gave her a bright smile and a grey and silver card on which she had penned the name 'Dunford'.

'Take the lift to the top floor and give this card to the receptionist who will meet you there.'

With heart stopping speed, Lindsey was wafted to the thirtieth storey, and disgorged into a vast grey-carpeted area dotted with steel and suede armchairs in silver-grey and black. The sombre colouring was relieved by bowls of yellow flowers—not a dying one in sight—and colourful pictures on the walls. Of the view there was not a glimpse, and seeing the many corridors that led off in all directions, she presumed that this area was in the centre of the building.

A man in his twenties came quickly towards her, his eyes on the card in her hand, and she held it out to him. Smiling a greeting, he took it from her and led her across the carpet to another lift.

'Don't tell me we're going down again!' she exclaimed, stepping in. 'I was definitely told to come to the top floor.'

'That's quite right. But we're going up.'

'*Up*?'

'One floor only.' His smile grew broader. 'It always fazes people the first time. But you'll soon see what I mean.'

The door slid back and Lindsey stepped out into a tinted world. Dumbstruck, she stopped and stared. She seemed to be standing in the centre of a suite of offices, with several doors open to show her that all the outside walls were made of glass, reinforced at regular intervals with bands of silver steel. But though the glass was tinted beige to minimise the glare, clever lighting simulated daylight inside.

'The chairman's office, and the offices of his personal staff, are all here. Mr Dunford is waiting for you.'

A silver birchwood door was opened and Lindsey found her hand being warmly pumped by a hard, calloused one.

'This is an unexpected pleasure, Mrs Ramsden,' Jack Dunford greeted her.

'I should have telephoned,' she began, 'but I——'

'Not at all. I much prefer talking face to face. Anyway, I'm pleased you've done as I asked.'

'How do you know I have?'

'If you hadn't, you *would* have telephoned!'

She couldn't restrain a slight smile and he returned it, his lined, pugnacious face softening.

'What are your plans now?' he asked.

'I haven't any. I'm not due back in New York till the end of September, though if I decide to remain in England permanently, I'll rejoin Universal TV.' She moved to the door and he stepped ahead of her and barred her way.

'Do you have time for a coffee?'

'Why?' Impatiently she ran a hand through her dark red hair. 'Do you want something else of me?'

'Yes.'

Despite herself, she laughed. 'You've certainly got gall. But you don't have to soften me up with a coffee. Just make your next outrageous demand!'

'I'd like you to return to live with Tim.'

Outraged, Lindsey glared at him. 'You've got a hell of a nerve!'

'I don't mean for real. Just to live in his house. I mean, if you're supposed to be together, you can hardly go on living separately, can you?'

'We've been doing it for over four years!'

'I realise that, but Carlo Malvini wasn't on the scene then. And he's no fool, you know. If you and Tim aren't sharing a home, he'll soon find out.'

'Did Tim put you up to this?'

Jack Dunford shook his head. 'He isn't as devious as I am. I'll do everything in my power to help him win this takeover, Mrs Ramsden.'

'Your loyalty's commendable,' Lindsey replied, 'but you are asking the impossible. I'm sure Tim would think the same.'

'I bet he wouldn't.'

'You'd lose your bet,' a hard voice exclaimed, and they both swung round to see the object of their discussion standing at the door, his face white with anger. 'You were out of order to ask it, Jack.' Tim glanced at Lindsey. 'Forget it, please.'

'Why are you dismissing it out of hand?' the older man intervened. 'When you became chairman and gave an interview to the Press, you were quizzed about your wife and said her career had temporarily taken her to the States. But if she returns to live with you—her love for you winning out against ambition—you'll get some great publicity out of it, which old Carlo is certain to be told about, and it would give you an advantage over Lawson.'

'The answer's still no!'

Tim sounded so dismissive that Lindsey could cheerfully have kicked him. Did he find even a temporary reunion so distasteful that he refused to consider it? The knowledge hurt her deeply, and it was an effort to keep it from showing. Without a word, she turned to leave, almost bumping into a young woman coming through the door.

Tall and soignée, her casual stone wool dress was no end-of-season Valentino bought in a sale, but one Lindsey had seen on the front cover of this month's *Vogue*. The heavy topaz and gold necklace around her throat, each tawny stone half an inch big, also had the stamp of serious money, as did an even larger topaz weighing down her right hand, while the snakeskin bag in her left one matched the low-heeled pumps on the elegantly narrow feet. But even had she worn a sack she would still have been ravishingly beautiful, for her creamy skin was velvet-smooth, her hair black and silky, and worn in a sleek, shoulder-length bob, the ends curling under softly. Everything about her spoke of leisure and care. No strap-hanging on public transport for this lovely creature, Lindsey thought wryly, and deliberately slowed her departure in the hope of discovering who she was.

'You haven't forgotten I'm waiting for you, have you Tim?' the girl asked in a husky, slightly foreign accent. 'I've been waiting in Reception for half an hour.'

'I'm sorry, Francesca.' Tim's warm smile was in sharp contrast to his cool manner with Lindsey. 'Something urgent's cropped up and I'll be busy for a while. Do you mind waiting a little longer?'

Francesca's dark, sloe-shaped eyes slid over Lindsey before returning to Tim. 'Will it make it easier for you if I go home?' she purred sweetly, laying a pink-tipped hand on his arm. 'After all, I'm seeing you tonight.'

'And you'll be seeing me for coffee in fifteen minutes,' Tim responded. 'Go into my office and wait for me.'

Smiling, though only at him, the girl departed on a waft of Shalimar, and Lindsey did her best to act unconcerned. So Tim *did* have a new girlfriend! And not only was she prettier than Patsy, but considerably more elegant.

It was easy to see why he had vetoed Jack Dunford's suggestion. Living with his wife again—albeit temporarily—wouldn't go down well with the lovely Francesca. Nor would it please Robert, she reflected, dismayed that until this second she hadn't given him a thought. It showed how fragile her feelings for him were.

Again she went to the door, but as she reached it the memory of Francesca's proprietorial manner towards

Tim goaded her into turning to the two men, though she looked only at Jack.

'If you honestly think it will help my husband win the bid for Malvini, I'm willing to do as you ask.' Only then did she glance at the tall, blond man standing behind him, her green eyes gleaming provocatively. 'Of course, if makes things awkward for you on a personal level, Tim...'

'I should imagine it will be more awkward for *you*,' he retorted coolly. 'You're the one on the verge of remarriage.'

'If your wife's prepared to play ball,' Jack Dunford put in quickly, 'you'll be mad to turn down the offer.'

'I wasn't going to turn it down. It's simply that I know my wife better than you do, and I can't help wondering why she is suddenly so amenable.'

'Because of your business record,' Lindsey stated, inwardly seething. 'I've always admired success in a man and I'm delighted you've finally achieved it.'

'I never realised you were the type to be turned on by success,' he drawled.

'That's what attracted me to Robert,' she lied, delighted to see Tim's mouth tighten.

'So that's why you're suddenly so helpful. In case Carlo Malvini learns of your relationship with him!'

'Let's say I don't want my presence to be a hindrance to Robert or you, and the best way of achieving that is to return to you, temporarily. Then the two of you can fight on even terms for the Italian company.'

'I couldn't have put it better myself,' Jack Dunford stated.

Tim glanced at him, then levelled a steady look at Lindsey. 'It appears to be an offer I can't refuse. I must admit I hadn't expected you to be so even-handed. I'd have thought you'd *want* Lawson to win.'

'I like a fair fight.'

'Then thank you. And I apologise for my early rudeness.'

'It was understandable,' she shrugged. 'We're both carrying painful baggage and it affects our actions.'

'How American you sound.' He gave a half-smile. 'I bet you have your own shrink!'

'I don't, as it happens, though perhaps both of us should have seen one.'

Tim's jaw clenched but he made no comment, turning instead to the man beside him. 'Well, Jack, what's next on your agenda for us?'

'Next we go to Smith Street.' Noting Lindsey's puzzlement, the man turned to her. 'Tim's home. I'd like you to move in as soon as possible.'

'Is that really necessary?' she asked, then shook her head. 'I'm sorry, of course it is.' She paused, unnerved by the prospect. 'I'd like to put it off until tomorrow, though. I want to talk to Robert first.'

'Naturally,' Tim said. 'And if you have second thoughts and change your mind, I'll understand.'

Was that because he himself was having second thoughts, thinking of Francesca perhaps? Lindsey wondered.

'I won't change my mind,' she asserted.

'I'll send my driver to pick you up. What time's best for you?'

'About noon.' She swung her gaze to Jack Dunford. 'I'd better go before you come up with something else for us to do!'

The lined face creased into a grin. 'How does the patter of tiny feet sound?'

'Terrible. *C'est dorer la pilule*!' she quoted in French.

'Come again?'

'It means "gilding the pill",' Tim translated brusquely. 'And the one you've already given us to swallow is hard enough, so no more jokes, please.'

It seemed business success had dimmed Tim's sense of humour, Lindsey thought as she went swiftly from the room, or did he dislike her so much that even in jest he recoiled from the very notion of her as the mother of his child?

The knowledge hurt her deeply but she knew she had to hide it. More than that, she had to forget it. He had forged a new career and a new life for himself, and she had no part in it.

She and Tim were only together temporarily. Once the bid was won—or lost—they would go their separate ways.

CHAPTER ELEVEN

'I've heard some outrageous suggestions in my time,' Robert exploded, 'but this one beats them all! I won't let you do it, Lindsey! Ring Ramsden and tell him you've changed your mind.'

'I can't do that,' Lindsey replied.

'Why not? If you go back to him you'll make me look an absolute fool.'

'I fail to see why.'

'Don't give me that. Dammit! What will my friends think?'

'The only thing your friends know about me is that I'm taking a seasonal break from television and helping out in your office.'

'You think that coming over from the States to do so doesn't suggest we're more than acquaintances?'

'I could have decided to work for you because I'm considering doing a documentary on the way certain big businesses are helping combat pollution. You yourself suggested it when you asked me to come here.'

Cornered, Robert changed tack.

'Why didn't you tell me earlier that you were thinking of going back to Ramsden?'

'Because I wasn't. It was only when Jack Dunford——'

Robert's expletive left Lindsey in little doubt as to his opinion of the man, and she could hardly blame him.

'I understand how you feel,' she soothed, 'but try to see it from my point of view.'

'All I see is that for the next few months you'll be living with the man you're supposed to be divorcing!'

'Living with him in name only. And you'll be so busy, the time will fly.'

'But you're helping his image by going back to him. That's what sticks in my gullet.'

'I could be harming *you* if I didn't.'

'You have everything worked out, haven't you?' Robert muttered. 'The only thing you can't resolve is how you feel about *me*. Or are you keeping me on the back burner until you find out whether Ramsden's willing to try again?'

Angrily, Lindsey jumped to her feet. The whole day had been emotionally fraught, and she could take no more.

'If you think I'm capable of behaving like that, I'm surprised you still want me. I was the one who walked away from my marriage. Tim didn't want me to go.'

'Does that mean he's always wanted you back? That he's used this takeover bid as a ploy?'

'Certainly not! He cares for someone else.'

'Who?'

'Someone called Francesca. I don't know her full name, just that she's beautiful, elegant, and Italian, I think.'

Robert visibly relaxed and, seeing it, Lindsey relaxed too.

'I don't blame you for being annoyed about all this,' she murmured. 'But we can still see each other if we're careful.'

'I'm beginning to loathe that word! I want to shout my love for you from the rooftops, not hide it.'

He rose too, and came over to her, standing so close that she could breathe in the aroma of the expensive aftershave he used. But to her shame all it did was remind her of Tim, and the memory of lying close to him, her lips upon his naked chest, sweat-stained after their love-making, and breathing in the musky scent of it.

'Can we at least have this coming weekend together?' Robert asked her.

Blankly she stared at him, then with an effort dragged her mind back to the present.

'I—I'm afraid not. I'm moving in with Tim tomorrow.'

'Great! Just tell me where in hell we're going to meet once you start playing house with him? At the back door—on the maid's night out?'

'That's a silly thing to say.'

'Answer me!'

'I've no idea where we'll meet. But I'll arrange something, I promise.' She was unexpectedly close to tears, and hearing her thickened voice, he was instantly contrite.

'Forgive me, darling, but this is such a crazy situation, I don't know where I'm at. Knowing you are going back to Ramsden has——'

'I'm not going back to him in the real sense of the word. I'm doing it because—because we loved one another once and I—I feel guilty at the way I left him.'

'You've never told me why you did.'

Robert didn't say this as a question, yet she knew it was; knew too that he had a right to know. Yet she couldn't bring herself to disclose it, a reaction which told her more about her current feelings for Tim than she cared to know. Or was it pride that was holding her back? After all, it didn't say much for her attractions that her husband of barely a year had turned so soon to a former girlfriend!

'It was a combination of many things,' she hedged. 'We came from different backgrounds, and it was mainly incompatibility.'

'But you blame yourself for the break-up more than you blame *him*?' Robert commented shrewdly.

'Yes, I do. I'm not the woman today that I was then. I was far less tolerant and much more opinionated. I guess I feel guilty for walking out the way I did, and I don't want the added burden of feeling guilty for losing him the chance to get Malvini—or losing you the chance of getting it either. By returning to him temporarily I'm levelling the situation.'

Robert sighed heavily but did not argue, and Lindsey allowed several seconds to tick by before she spoke.

'I'd like to give up this apartment, Robert. I won't be requiring it for the next few months and——'

'I'll pay the rent,' he interrupted tersely.

'I don't want you to!'

'Why not? It's such a little thing for me to do for you; for God's sake don't refuse me.'

Although unhappy with the idea, she gave in, unwilling to anger or hurt him further. As he came closer and stroked her hair, she sensed a difference in his attitude, and realising where it might lead, she eased slowly away from him, trying to make the move casual.

'How selfish of me to keep you here so late when you've had such a long day. If I don't watch out, I'll start feeling guilty about *you*!'

'So you should,' he rejoined. 'But not for the reasons you think. You're putting me on hold and I know it.'

'It's the only way I can get through the next few months. Moving into Tim's home won't be easy for me.'

'I'm aware of that, and I'll do my best not to make it any harder for you.' Robert moved to the door. 'At least you didn't plead a headache—so I suppose I should be grateful for that!'

'Grateful?'

'That you credit me with *some* sensitivity!'

'Robert, I——'

'No, darling, don't try to placate me. Let's just agree that tonight was the worst since we met. After this, things can only get better!'

As the front door closed behind him, she was deeply sorry that she had been forced to hurt him. Yet she was also sorry for herself, aware that the months ahead, when she would be sharing a home with Tim, would inevitably open old and painful wounds. But Tim mustn't know it; must never guess she still loved him with all her heart.

Oh, God! What had she thought?

Shaking, she collapsed on to a chair, horrified by her admission. It wasn't true, of course. All she felt for him was desire. It definitely wasn't love. It couldn't be. He had always had the ability to arouse her, and his new maturity and success had simply acted upon her emotions like a strong aphrodisiac.

But supposing he recognised her vulnerability and took advantage of it? He might dislike her but that didn't mean he'd be averse to taking her to bed. Like most men, Tim didn't need to be in love to have sex with a woman. Patsy was proof of *that*.

Agitatedly she paced the floor. She had to make it clear to him that sex was out, and if he attempted to so much as kiss her she would leave him immediately.

Feeling calmer, she undressed and had a hot bath. Though it relaxed her, she was in no mood to sleep, and she switched on the television to watch an old Grace Kelly movie. But the fairy-tale romance only served to remind her how different her own marriage had been, and she turned it off.

I wasn't kind enough to Tim, she acknowledged soberly. I took him away from his home and his environment. I wanted to fashion him into someone different and never gave a thought to what *he* wanted to be. No wonder he turned to Patsy. She made it plain she loved him for what he was. And I'm damn sure Francesca does the same!

With an angry thump on the pillow, Lindsey buried her face in it and pulled the sheet over her head.

CHAPTER TWELVE

NEXT morning, halfway through her packing, the doorbell rang.

Assuming it was the chauffeur calling to collect her, Lindsey opened the door, taken aback to see a young man on the threshold, carrying a small wicker basket.

'Miss Phillips?' At her nod, he handed it to her and left.

She stood gazing at it, then nearly dropped it as the basket suddenly moved in her hand. She heard a plaintive cry, and with a gasp inched up the lid and peered inside. Bright blue eyes stared back at her, and she set the basket on the floor and carefully lifted out a cream and brown Siamese kitten.

'You beautiful little darling,' she cooed, holding it close and resting her cheek on the silky fur.

The kitten gave a protesting miaow and struggled to be free, and Lindsey set it on the floor. As she did, she found a card attached to the inside of the basket, and taking it out, saw it was from Robert.

'You left Angus because of me,' she read; 'now you're leaving me for Ramsden. So I'm sending you another cat to remind you why you came back to England. I've called him Bruce, and when *you* do, I hope you'll think of me, because, like Robert the Bruce and his spider, I'm not giving up!'

It was a humorous note, yet she detected the seriousness behind it, and with a sudden pang picked up the cat and hugged it close again.

'Miaow!' it cried, and jumping free, darted across the room and up the curtain.

'That's not very friendly,' she chided. 'Come down and I'll give you something to drink.'

Ignoring her, the kitten clawed its way higher, finally reaching the pelmet board and perching on the top of it, tail swinging.

'Come down, Bruce!' she ordered.

For answer, the kitten settled itself on the pelmet ledge and wrapped its tail around its legs.

'I can see I'll have to resort to bribery.' Smiling, Lindsey went into the kitchen, filled a saucer with milk and carried it into the living-room. Setting it on the floor, she tapped the rim to attract the kitten's attention, but he yawned delicately and remained where he was.

'Be like that, then,' she declared. 'You'll just have to stay there till you get tired of it.'

She went on with her packing, and had almost finished when there was another ring at the door. Expecting to see Robert following on his gift, she ran to open it, her warm smile dying as she found herself staring at Tim. But a Tim from the past. In grey trousers and unstructured, lighter grey jacket, his hair slightly windblown, he was more like the man she had married.

She swallowed hard. 'I—I thought you were sending your driver?'

'I felt it would look better if I collected you personally. It's what I'd do if our reconciliation was genuine.'

'You'd better come in and wait. I'm not quite ready.'

Leaving him in the sitting-room, she went into the bathroom and hurriedly emptied the cabinet. She hadn't yet packed her books, but there was no time; she would return for them later.

Rejoining Tim, she found him surveying Bruce, still perched on top of the curtains.

'Did the cat go with the apartment?' he enquired.

'No. But it goes with *me*. Robert sent him—as a gift to remember him by.'

'I see.'

His words were non-committal, and Lindsey had no idea what he was thinking. Yet once upon a time she would have known merely by looking at him. Now she couldn't even begin to guess. All she knew was that he had a beautiful Italian girlfriend. How many other women had there been in his life since Patsy? Hastily she thrust aside the thought.

'I didn't know you were a cat-lover,' Tim went on.

'I wasn't—until I inherited Angus. When I moved into my apartment in New York, I found him there. The previous owner just walked off and left him.'

'And you walked out on him too.'

Lindsey's heart thumped. Was Tim aware he had said the same of her behaviour to himself? Pretending not to have noticed it, she shrugged.

'He's being spoiled rotten by the Wengers—they're an elderly couple who lived opposite me.'

'If you intend settling here, why didn't you bring him with you?'

'Because of the six months' quarantine,' she lied, having no intention of letting him know how indecisive she was about Robert. 'He's an old cat and would have hated being with strangers. He always stayed with the Wengers when I had to go out of town, so he's used to them.' Tilting her head back, she stared at the kitten. 'The little beast's determined to stay up there.' She turned to Tim, a sudden thought striking her. 'You won't mind, will you?'

'If he stays on the pelmet?'

'Of course not. I mean if I bring him to your house. I know you're a dog man and——'

'I don't object to cats—if they keep out of my way.'

'Right now he's keeping out of *my* way too,' Lindsey said grimly, and climbing on to a chair, reached for him. 'Come on, Bruce, there's a good boy.'

The kitten miaowed and backed away.

'If I had a name like Bruce, I'd protest too,' Tim commented, amusement in his voice.

Lindsey was instantly defensive. 'Robert chose it, and I like it.' Jumping off the chair, she bent and tapped the saucer of milk. 'Come on, kitty.'

But the cream and brown Siamese stayed exactly where he was.

Tim strode over to the curtain and looked up, arms folded across his chest. 'Get down, Nuisance,' he ordered tersely, 'or I'll be after you with a broomstick!'

With a soft cry the kitten took a flying leap on to his shoulder, clawing at his jacket to steady itself. Tim caught hold of the ball of fur and gingerly pulled it free before setting it beside the saucer.

'I'll fetch your cases,' he went on, and walked into the bedroom.

Lindsey bent to pick up the kitten, and seeing her hand reach out, he dived under the table.

'Nice Bruce,' she wheedled, scrabbling under the table after him. 'I just want to put you in your basket.'

'That's guaranteed to keep him under the table forever!' Tim commented, returning with her luggage, and she hurriedly straightened and smoothed her tumbling hair away from her face.

'You talk as if the little beast understands what I'm saying.'

'Animals understand tone, and the tone of your voice as you mentioned basket alerted him to the fact that it's a key word and it worries you. Probably because you envisage trouble getting him into it!'

'Thanks for the lesson in animal psychology.'

'Any time.' Tim sauntered close to the table. 'Come on, Nuisance,' he commanded again, and clapped his hands.

To Lindsey's intense annoyance, the kitten leapt into his arms for the second time, and Tim couldn't restrain a grin.

'You can call him Bruce if you want, but it seems he prefers Nuisance.'

'It certainly suits him,' she muttered, then couldn't help laughing.

Tim joined in, then placed the kitten in his wicker basket ready for the journey to Chelsea.

It was a short drive from the apartment to his four-storey Regency house, and as they entered the rectangular hall she gazed around with interest. It was a far cry from the walk-up apartment where they had spent their married life. The floor was grey and gold veined marble, though the curving stairs, with their elegant wrought-iron banisters, were carpeted in crimson, giving warmth to an otherwise austere entrance. The walls were lacquered white, and a black and red Chinese lacquer table supported a white porcelain bowl of red roses.

'Do you live here by yourself?' The question slipped out, and she blushed. What a stupid thing to have asked. He'd hardly be living here with Francesca.

'I have a housekeeper and her husband,' Tim replied. 'Henry and Mary Parker. He's my chauffeur-cum-odd-job-man.' He moved towards the stairs. 'I'll show you to your room.'

Clutching the wicker basket, Lindsey followed.

'The master suite and my study,' he stated, pointing to two rooms on the first floor. Then they went up a second flight where there were two further bedrooms, each with a bathroom.

'There's another floor above this,' he stated.

'The servants' quarters?' she commented. 'Or are they still below stairs?'

'Still waging your class war, Lindsey?'

'Sorry, that was a stupid thing to say.'

'You're actually apologising?'

'I do when I'm wrong.'

'You *have* changed.'

Her mouth tightened. 'If you're going to make snide remarks——'

'I'm not. You aren't the only one who says stupid things.'

Mollified, she followed him into a bedroom domi-
nated by an impressive four-poster, its pillows and
squashy duvet covered with finest Egyptian cotton, lace-
encrusted. The smoky blues and coral colours of the
drapes and carpet complemented the mahogany of the
small pie-crust tables that stood either side of the bed,
and the Regency sofa-table—bearing a silver-framed
stand-up mirror—that served as a dressing-table.

'I hired an interior designer,' Tim volunteered. 'It's a
bit too *Homes and Gardens* for my taste, but I'm hoping
it will wear in.'

'And if it doesn't?'

'I'm putting my faith in Nuisance!'

Chuckling, Lindsey opened the wicker basket. The
kitten jumped out and started bounding round the room,
falling flat on its face when its paws became entangled
in the fringe of an Oriental rug by the window. Thank
heaven for the cat. Without him, the tension caused by
moving here would have been unbearable.

'I'll leave you to settle in,' Tim spoke from the
doorway. 'If there's anything you require, let me know.'

She marvelled at the formality between them. He
sounded like a hotel proprietor talking to a guest, instead of to the woman who had shared his bed and
aroused his passion! But that was in the past, and today
his bed held the lovely Francesca.

Not while I'm living here, it won't! she vowed mutin-
ously, and, catching sight of her frowning face in the
mirror, was furious to be thinking this. Tim was no more
likely to ask Francesca to the house than *she* would invite
Robert. The only reason she was here was because they
were pretending they were happily married—which the
appearance of Francesca and Robert would un-
doubtedly negate!

'Why are you frowning?' Tim quizzed.

'It just came home to me that living here won't be
easy for either of us.'

'Easier for me than you, Lindsey. I have something to gain from it, but you've had to put your personal life on hold and——'

'So have you,' she intervened. 'I hope Francesca's as understanding as Robert?'

'Unfortunately not. When a woman is driven by her emotions, logic takes a back seat!'

How right he was, Lindsey mused as she unpacked her clothes. If logic had governed her years ago, she might have fought to save her marriage. She shook her head. No, she had done the correct thing. Well, the only thing right for *her*. Liberated woman though she was, she could never overlook adultery, and knowing Tim had been unfaithful had ruined any chance of reconciliation.

Yet now she was back with him, which went to show how events could mould one's actions. How would she feel staying here, part of his life again, yet emotionally apart from it? Could she act the dutiful wife successfully? Could she cope with business dinners and the many other duties that fell upon the wife of such a successful man?

The kitten miaowed, and she picked it up. At least this farce with Tim would prepare her for life with Robert! A full dress rehearsal for the future, with only a single change of cast—Robert in place of Tim. She hugged the cat cat closer, wishing she could see Robert as her lover, her husband. But she saw only the past and a blond-haired man.

'Call Robert and say you'll marry him,' she muttered, but as she reached for the telephone her hand dropped to her side. She couldn't do it. Not yet.

Painful tears dripped on to the kitten's furry back, and with a whimper of protest he wriggled free of her hold and darted out of the room and down the stairs.

'Bruce! Nuisance!' she cried, chasing after him, worried he might make a mess on the plush red carpet.

As he reached the first landing, Tim stepped from his study and scooped him up with one hand.

'I think he wants to go out,' she ventured breathlessly. 'Is it safe to let him into the garden?'

'Perfectly. It's walled in.' The kitten miaowed plaintively and Tim tweaked his ear. 'I'll put him out for you. Have you finished unpacking?'

'Almost. Why?'

'We're lunching at the Savoy.'

'Why?'

'As a show of togetherness. Jack's idea.'

'I figured it was. He doesn't waste time, does he?'

Tim's smile was cool. 'To quote Macbeth, "If it were done when 'tis done, then t'were well it were done quickly." And the sooner people know we're together, the better.'

'What exactly did you tell your friends regarding our separation?' Lindsey asked, pausing halfway back to the second floor.

Tim moved further forward, and the sun, shining through the window behind him, turned his hair to gold. 'That our marriage hit a bad patch and we decided to live apart while we were forging our careers.'

'What's the story going to be now?'

'That when you returned from the States we realised we still loved each other. The simpler our explanation, the more likely it is to be believed. I'll tell my parents the truth, of course. Incidentally, we're going to Evebury this weekend.'

Lindsey felt a pang of apprehension, recollecting how uncomfortable she had always felt there. 'Do I *have* to go?'

'It isn't only a social visit. Ramsden Engineering is still there and I like to visit it as often as I can. Since Semperton Trust took it over, it's been greatly enlarged and is one of our showpieces.'

'Our?' she queried.

'Semperton's.'

'You've really become a company man!' she exclaimed.

'I give it my total loyalty. That's the only way I can work.'

Ashamed for having baited him, she apologised. 'I know. I was just teasing. But I still don't see why I have to go to Evebury with you.'

'Because my parents live there, and eventually it will be my home.' Tim's jaw tightened, showing the patrician bone-structure. 'I assure you I'd be happier going there alone, but the whole purpose of this exercise is to show we're back together, and Jack thinks it's important for us to be seen together in my home town.'

'Do I have to visit the factory with you and charm the men?'

'No. And I can do without your sarcasm. If you can't enter this charade wholeheartedly, don't let's begin it. We won't convince people otherwise.'

'You're right. I'm just being bloody-minded. Sorry.'

'Is it that time of the month?'

Startled, she stared at him, colour flooding her face at the unexpected intimacy of his question.

'No,' she retorted, 'it isn't. I'm often bloody-minded, in case you've forgotten.'

'I haven't.' Faint humour edged his voice. 'But I'd call it strong-minded.'

'Thanks.' She hesitated. 'What—what reason will you give when we split?'

'The demands of your career. Unless you can think of something better?'

'No, that one's fine.' She moved up the stairs.

'Our table at the Savoy is booked for one,' he called. 'I'd like us to leave at twelve-thirty.'

At twenty-five past, she made her way downstairs, a narrow skirted suit in yellow silk showing her shapely figure to advantage.

Tim, in dark pinstriped suit, stood in the hall and openly appraised her. 'Your fashion sense has certainly changed. You used only to like way-out gear.'

'I still have a few items in my wardrobe.' She turned to the stairs.

'God, no!'

Hiding a grin, she followed him out to the gleaming grey Jaguar, relieved to see his chauffeur at the wheel; she still felt ill at ease alone with Tim.

Twenty minutes later they were being shown to their table in the River Room, a progress frequently halted by Tim pausing to answer a jovial greeting. He was punctilious at introducing her as his wife, and though she watched to see any reaction from his business friends— for this was what she judged them to be—they were too sophisticated to show any.

It was strange to be at Tim's side, and she noticed how at ease he was, how friendly his manner. It was no pose either, but the genuine man; the Tim of old, who had captivated her.

Only as they sat down at their table did his face and manner harden perceptibly, until the man of the past disappeared and the present model, always so cool and controlled with her, faced her.

'Well, that wasn't too embarrassing for you, was it?' he commented.

'I'm surprised Mr Dunford wasn't here to make sure we played our parts properly!'

'Jack knows when to keep in the background. He didn't want our first appearance together to look stage-managed.'

'Did he give you any coaching? You gave a wonderful performance.'

'You didn't do badly yourself. But then, you *are* a performer, aren't you?'

She gave him a sharp glance but discerned no gibe. He was merely stating a fact.

'Some of the documentaries you've made have been shown over here,' he went on, 'and I saw a couple of them. They were excellent.'

'Thank you for saying so.'

'Why shouldn't I? I always knew you weren't a background girl and that one day you'd be a success.'

How calmly he spoke about it; as if she were another of his business acquaintances and not the wife who had walked out on him. Stop that, she ordered herself. You had good reason for walking out, and don't forget it.

A waiter approached with the menu, and they gave their order, Lindsey glad to concentrate on something other than Tim.

'The food here is always good,' he informed her.

'I know. I've eaten here with Robert.'

'Of course.'

They both fell silent, and she sipped the wine Tim had chosen, noticing he was only drinking mineral water. 'Don't tell me you've become a teetotaller!'

'Only at lunch. I have to go to quite a few business ones, and I find that alcohol impairs my thinking. I eat lightly too, during the day. There's nothing more soporific than a big meal, don't you think?'

'An American business lunch rarely lasts longer than an hour,' she smiled, 'and you are so busy talking shop that what you put into your mouth is of relatively little importance!'

'Is that why you're so thin?'

Instantly she felt gaunt, all angles and sharp bones, unlike the curvaceous Francesca, and it was an effort to look uncaring.

'Don't you know the old saying, Tim? A woman can never be too thin and a man never too rich!'

'You can't have changed so much that you believe that rubbish!'

'Of course not. But to be honest, the camera always adds pounds to your appearance, and——'

'You have nothing to worry about,' he cut across her. 'You're a very beautiful woman, and a few pounds either way makes no difference.'

The arrival of their first course—smoked salmon, thinly sliced as only the Savoy could do it—saved her from having to find an answer to this, and by the time the waiter had gone she found it easy to switch the focus of the conversation on to Tim.

'Do you enjoy heading such a huge company?'

'Very much. But it isn't one huge company—it's a conglomerate of many different ones, ranging from oil, steel, timber and engineering to food, supermarkets, and software.'

'Don't tell me you run all of them!'

'I won't. I have an excellent team of managers who do the running. My job is to watch the profitability. I only step in if it starts slipping.'

'You must have worked terribly hard to get to the top so quickly.' She saw the quizzical gleam in the grey eyes facing her, and vouchsafed firmly, 'I mean it. I'm not the type to flatter.'

'That much I remember!'

Only as they were finishing their coffee did Tim mention that he would not be in to dinner.

'I've a speaking engagement, I'm afraid.'

Was he lying? His expression was unreadable and she had no intention of asking him.

'In that case, you won't mind if I have dinner with Robert, will you? We'll be discreet and go somewhere quiet and unfashionable.'

'Thanks.' Tim hesitated. 'I'll have my secretary make up a diary for the engagements I'd like you to attend with me. If you require any additional clothes, please bill them to my account.'

'That won't be necessary.'

'It's money I've *earned*, Lindsey. I know you never liked me to take anything from my trust fund.'

'I wouldn't think the same today,' she answered without thinking, and could have kicked herself when she saw him digest that comment.

'You have indeed changed.'

'Not where morals and ethics are concerned.'

A nerve twitched at the side of Tim's mouth, and he glanced at his wristwatch. 'Time for me to leave. I'm chairing a meeting in ten minutes. After Parker has dropped me off, he can take you home or wherever you want to go.'

When she was finally alone in the car, she asked the chauffeur to take her to St James's Park, then told him not to wait. She wanted to be alone with her thoughts, and where better to mull over them than this most gracious of green areas in the capital?

Watching the ducks and swans gliding across the sunlit water of the lake, she reflected that her lunch with Tim had gone quite well. There had been a few awkward moments, but given the circumstances it was not surprising.

One thing she had learned, though. She had to guard her tongue. If she didn't it could give away her feelings for Tim. And what a laugh he would have if he discovered she had never stopped loving him.

CHAPTER THIRTEEN

LINDSEY found it easier than she had anticipated to settle down in Tim's house; the only drawback was having too much time on her hands. The house was run with super efficiency by Mrs Parker and a full-time daily, leaving Lindsey to arrange the flowers—her only household chore.

She had rarely been idle in her life, and couldn't begin to guess what rich women did with their time, apart from shopping for clothes and lunching with friends—their children, of course, usually taken care of by a nanny. At least if she married Robert she could continue with her career. There was no way she would allow herself to merely be a suitable appendage for him on social occasions—as had happened to her with Tim in the two weeks since she had moved in with him.

His intention of taking her to Evebury their first weekend together had been scuppered when Robert had increased his bid for Malvini, necessitating Tim's calling a meeting of his board of directors before launching a counter-bid, and they were going down this Friday instead.

At least she could be herself there. Pretence was not natural for her, and she found it difficult to parry the personal questions from the Press who had, as predicted by Jack Dunford, latched on to their reconciliation.

Her first encounter with the tabloids had been an ordeal, partly because she had been taken unawares.

Accompanying Tim to a dinner at Claridge's, in aid of Save the Woodlands, she couldn't help comparing it with the rare outings they had shared during their brief marriage. Because she had wanted to show his parents they could live well on their joint salary, she had persuaded him not to touch the money in his trust fund, and consequently they had sat in the 'gods' at the theatre, and eaten in restaurants noted for their cheapness rather than their food.

Even my clothes were cheap and cheerful, she mused, her mind's eye visualising the hotch-potch of colourful ethnic garments that had once been her choice. But not any more. Tonight she was drop-dead sophistication.

Black silk jersey draped itself around her body, the sleeves long, the neckline only low enough to show the curve of her milk-white shoulders. But the soft folds drew attention to the gently curving line of her hips and her handspan waist, so that when the eye travelled higher the lushness of her full, firm breasts came as a shock.

She had piled her thick auburn hair on top of her head, and it emphasised her high cheekbones and voluptuous mouth. But she had allowed a few tendrils to drift free, and they softened the severe style. She wore no jewellery, having concluded that the other women guests were likely to be decked out in the real thing, and that if she couldn't compete on equal terms she wasn't going to enter the fray.

'You're very pensive, Lindsey.'

Tim broke the silence and she turned to him. God, he was handsome. The blackness of his dinner suit deepened the blondness of his hair, and it gleamed like a golden helmet, owing, she was pretty certain, to the vigorous brushing he had given it to ensure the errant wave in the front didn't break free and fall across his forehead. She had loved it when it had, and her hand itched to reach out and ruffle the smoothness.

'I was thinking how different tonight is from the way we used to go out,' she admitted, marvelling that her words bore no resemblance whatsoever to the mad thoughts rushing round in her head. 'They were fun evenings, weren't they?'

'Only in retrospect. Memories often play us for a fool.'

'I guess you're right,' she confirmed lightly, chilled by the coolness of his voice and hurt by the words. Didn't he look back with pleasure on *any* of the things they had done together?

To her relief she noticed their car was slowing, and she leaned forward expectantly.

The brilliance of flashlights blinded her when she stepped on to the pavement, and she was too startled to make any sense of the barrage of questions being hurled at her.

'If you put your questions one at a time, we'll do our best to answer them,' Tim said smoothly, putting an arm around her waist and drawing her closer to him.

Lindsey tensed, her pulses racing as she caught the faint scent of his aftershave, and the more intimate scent of the man himself. Against her will she was again wafted back to the past: to sunlit walks in the park, candle-lit dinners and passion-filled nights. Scared of the longing she felt, it was all she could do to resist throwing off his hand and running away.

Sensing her panic, and misinterpreting it, Tim tightened his hold.

'I know this is tough for you,' he whispered in her ear, 'but do your best to look madly in love with me!'

Forcing a smile to lips that seemed to be sealed together with SuperGlue, she nestled shyly against his shoulder. Despite looking as though he didn't have a spare ounce of flesh, he was comfortable to lean upon, his strength and height diminishing her own tall slenderness and making her feel safe and secure. Odd that she never felt this way with Robert. But then she didn't love Robert the way she—— Stop it! she warned herself. The past is over and there's another woman in Tim's life. He may be holding you close but he's only playing a part. It's Francesca he wants, and don't forget it.

'When did you return to your husband?' one of the reporters flung at her.

'Shortly after I came back from America.'

'Did he court you all over again?' a hard faced young woman with enormous spectacles demanded.

'We courted each other. This is the era of equality.'

Lindsey's answer brought a ripple of laughter, and a squeeze of approval from Tim.

'How about giving us a kiss for the front page?' a photographer called.

This is the stuff of nightmares, Lindsey thought, knowing that if her lips touched Tim's he would realise he could still arouse her. Deliberately she focused on the photographer.

'You'll have to introduce yourself first. I never kiss men I don't know!'

There was a roar of laughter and, taking advantage of the bonhomie it engendered, Tim swiftly propelled her through the crowd and into the hotel.

'You handled them like a trouper,' he congratulated her.

'I agree,' stated Jack Dunford, who had materialised from nowhere. 'It was a perfect performance.'

'I didn't know you were coming to the dinner.' Tim eyed him in surprise.

'I'm not. I just came to see how well you both did with the Press on your first "outing".' He grinned at Lindsey. 'I bet the shot of you leaning against Tim's shoulder will be the one most used.'

He was proved correct, and it resulted in requests to interview her alone, with even the upmarket papers joining the clamour.

Robert did not take kindly to the mass of publicity, and wasted no time voicing his disapproval when he saw her. She had only seen him twice since moving to Chelsea, and each time they had dined at a small restaurant in Barnes, its proprietor chef an old schoolfriend of his, guaranteed to be discreet.

On both occasions she had driven herself to the restaurant, and the last time Robert had promised to find another venue nearer to Chelsea.

'I'll wait for you to call me,' were his parting words. 'Don't make me wait too long.'

This morning she had guiltily realised that it was more than a week since they had spoken. I'll call him later, she promised herself as she shopped for flowers and returned home to replenish the vases, a weekly task she thoroughly enjoyed.

Tim had been out most evenings, not returning until well after midnight, when she was long since in bed. Because of it she made a point of seeing him at breakfast each day, and noticed he did not explain where he spent his time. Yet today, before leaving for his office, he had announced he would be in to dinner, and, remembering that when he had brought her here he had said his house was too like a set piece, she decided to make it look more lived in.

At that moment Nuisance—he refused to answer to anything else—padded into the living-room and flexed his claws against a brocaded settee.

'Stop it!' she cried, scooping him up. 'We don't need claw marks to make the house look lived in. I know far better ways.'

To prove it, she decided to soften the formality of the room by repositioning the settees and the armchairs, removing the carefully composed clutter of china and silver ornaments on the side tables and replacing them with bowls of fruit and nuts, and scattering a pile of magazines on the low stool in front of the fireplace.

'Much better,' she approved out loud, then laughed as Nuisance completed the picture by jumping on to an armchair and curling up on the cushion.

The ring of the doorbell startled her, and a moment later Mrs Parker informed her that Miss Francesca Belloti wished to see her.

Lindsey was startled enough to show it, and the housekeeper's expression of discomfiture made it clear she knew what role the Italian girl played in Tim's life.

The poor woman probably thinks Francesca's come here to tear out my hair!

'Please show her in,' she said composedly.

The Italian girl was even more stunning on second viewing, clothed in emerald-green that made her black hair blacker, her creamy skin creamier, her jewels today cabochon rubies and pearls. Real, Lindsey knew, and, recollecting that at first sight she had guessed Francesca to have serious money, she now amended it to *very* serious money.

'Forgive me for arriving without telephoning you first,' the girl proclaimed in her prettily accented voice, 'but I didn't know if I'd have time to get here. I'm leaving for Rome in two hours.'

Lindsey smiled and waited, not sure what was coming. What did shook her rigid.

'I wanted to return these.' A pink-tipped hand dipped into an emerald-green snakeskin purse and withdrew a pair of gold cufflinks. 'Tim's,' she announced baldly. 'I only found them this morning. He dressed in such a rush the other night, he must have forgotten them.'

A wave of pure, unadulterated rage engulfed Lindsey, and as it receded, the pretence that she didn't love him went with it. Of course she did! She was madly, crazily in love with him, and would never love anyone else.

'I was going to put them in an envelope and send them to Tim's secretary,' Francesca went on, 'but important things often get leaked to the Press these days, and I felt it was safer for me to bring them here.'

'Wise of you,' Lindsey agreed, marvelling at her ability to control her voice. How could she speak so softly when all she wanted to do was scream and shout? 'How long will you be in Rome?'

'Until Tim has won control of Malvini. If I continue staying here, he will insist on visiting me, and I'm terribly scared someone will see him. I told him the other night that I was leaving but he didn't believe me.' Francesca's silky black hair swung upon her shoulders as she leaned forward, scenting the air with Femme. 'I love him very much and I'd be desolated if our relationship leaked out and Carlo Malvini got to hear about it. He is such a rigid man, that one. If he had his way, no one would be allowed to divorce, and men and women who loathed one another would be forced to stay together.'

'Many people agree with him.'

'Fine. But let them not dictate what others should do.' Francesca sighed. 'I haven't called Tim to say goodbye in case he persuades me not to go. I am so weak-willed where he is concerned.' Tears glimmered in the dark eyes, and the girl dabbed at them with a lacy handkerchief. 'I suppose you'll part as soon as the battle is won?'

It was only with an effort that Lindsey hid the pleasure she felt at the question, which showed that the Italian girl was nowhere near as sure of Tim as she was making out.

'I'm not sure exactly *when* I'll leave. I shouldn't think Tim will want to make our parting too obvious. You know how malicious the Press can be. If they feel they have had the wool pulled over their eyes, they could give him a hard time.'

'I hadn't thought of that. Still, as soon as Carlo is out of the way, I can come back and be the woman Tim turned to when he learned you were planning to leave him again!'

'Ever considered writing romantic fiction?' Lindsey asked drily.

'I don't have the imagination.' Francesca took the question seriously. 'I could only write about things I know, and Tim would be furious if I disclosed the intimacies between us, if you follow what I mean?'

'Loud and clear. You really don't need to lay such vociferous claim to him, Miss Belloti. I stopped being interested in him years ago.'

'Oh, dear, I wasn't implying you were trying to come between us. Please forgive me.'

'It's already forgotten. Now, if you'll excuse me, I have to go out.'

With another flurry of apology, Francesca left, and as the front door closed behind her Lindsey slumped low in the chair, unable to think, yet painfully able to feel.

CHAPTER FOURTEEN

IT WAS after eight when Tim arrived home, by which time Lindsey had buried her pain deep inside her. She was good at doing that; not surprising when she had done it successfully for nearly five years.

Lounging on a settee, casual in black silk trousers and pink chiffon blouse that increased the lustre of her auburn hair, she studied him from beneath her lashes. Although he'd had a long, hard day he managed to look as immaculate as an Armani advert—a fact that would have irritated her once, but which she now saw as an inherent part of him. Put him to digging ditches and he'd still have the same clean-cut aura! He came nearer and she noticed his face was lined with fatigue; not surprising given that he was playing the adoring husband while being Francesca's passionate lover. Still, he'd be able to rest now!

'You look exhausted,' she commented, as he went to the drinks tray and poured a tot of whisky.

'I've had a tough week. Lawson's fighting tooth and nail to get control of the Italian company.'

'I'm sure he's saying the same thing about you!'

'Probably.' He reached for the soda siphon. 'I suppose the showdown can't come soon enough for you?'

'For you too, I imagine.'

'Not really. I enjoy a good clean fight.'

'I was referring to the charade of our "happy marriage".'

'Oh, I see.' His shoulders lifted. 'It doesn't bother me.'

'Francesca wouldn't like to hear you say *that*,' Lindsey said, and Tim went motionless. 'She was here this morning and asked me to tell you she left for Rome this morning, and won't be returning until the takeover is finished.'

Tim splashed soda into his glass. 'May I get you a drink?'

'I'll wait till dinner.' Irritated by his cool reaction, Lindsey would not let the subject drop. 'She also said that when she told you about it the other night, you didn't believe her.'

If he noticed the words 'other night', he gave no sign of it. 'Of course I believed her—and she knew it. Seems extraordinary for her to have come here to tell you.'

'She actually came to leave these.' Calmly Lindsey pointed to the little table beside her, where gold cufflinks gleamed beneath the light of a jade lamp. 'You left them in her apartment.'

Nonchalantly Tim slipped them into his pocket, infuriating Lindsey by his lack of embarrassment.

'I think Francesca decamped out of pique,' he drawled. 'I told her we should cool things for the moment, and this is her answer. She doesn't like sharing me with you.'

Lindsey's green eyes flashed. 'I hope she doesn't think we——'

'Not at all.' His denial was unflatteringly swift. 'What I meant was that Francesca wants my entire spare time, and right now that's not possible.'

'You don't seem upset by her departure.'

'I'm not. I know her well enough to take these little things in my stride. She'll come back when her temper has cooled.'

'Are you going to marry her?'

An arched eyebrow rose. 'Does that mean you care? Or do you want me off your conscience before you marry Lawson?'

'You aren't on my conscience, Tim. You never were.'

'I'm glad to hear it.' His tone was easy, his demeanour relaxed. 'You did me a favour by leaving me. If you hadn't, I might not be where I am today.'

'Me too,' Lindsey endorsed, smiling as her hopes shrivelled and her heart seemed to lose its reason for beating. 'Both of us have it all, don't we? A career we love, another person we love——' she stopped short, as if by accident. 'I assume you do love Francesca?'

'I wouldn't marry her if I didn't. She'll make a perfect wife. She's beautiful, amusing, and has an impeccable Euro background. Her mother's French and her father's an Italian prince!'

That should please Mrs Ramsden, Lindsey thought. 'I didn't realise you were so calculating,' was what she said. 'You never used to be.'

'I never used to be a lot of things. Change is a part of growing up.'

'Not all change is for the better.'

Tim sipped his whisky. 'I'd have thought *any* change you saw in me was for the better. You were always having a go at me for one thing or the other.'

'Was I really such a harridan?'

'Let's say you tended to concentrate on my faults rather than my virtues!'

With hindsight, she knew his comment was justified, and wondered if battered ego had made him vulnerable to Patsy.

'You aren't the only one to have changed,' she declared abruptly. '*I've* changed too.'

'I know. Your rough edges have smoothed and you no longer wave the rebel's flag.'

'I'll still never be a conformist!'

'Good. Sheep are boring. You also have more panache,' he unexpectedly added.

'Thanks for nothing. The dictionary defines that as swagger.'

'Sorry, I forgot you were a pedant; in that respect you're still the same! What I meant was that you've acquired polish and style.'

'Success helps,' she murmured, raking a pink tipped hand through her thick auburn hair. 'It has done the same to you.'

'How nice we're being to one another,' Tim observed drily.

'Why shouldn't we be? We aren't enemies. What's past is past.'

'Good of you to say so.' The dryness was even more pronounced. 'After all, I've delayed your marriage to Lawson.'

So Tim thought she definitely intended marrying Robert. She hadn't actually told him so, but maybe it was what he wanted to believe. After all, it was tidier to have one's ex-wife safely married than floating free. Should she admit she hadn't yet decided? Not sure what to do, she wandered across to the drinks tray.

'I think I'll have something after all.'

Fortified by a vodka and tonic, she suddenly found herself asking the question that had niggled her for years. 'I was surprised you didn't divorce me after the required two years' separation. I took it for granted you'd want to marry Patsy.'

Tim stared into his glass. 'You'd have liked that, wouldn't you? Then your leaving me would have been justified.'

'Justified?' Lindsey questioned angrily. 'That presupposes I felt guilty for going to the States—and I didn't. You're the one who should feel *that*.'

'You must be joking! If you'd given us a chance to talk things through, we——'

'How could we talk things through when you stormed out that night and didn't come back?'

'I wanted to give us both a chance to cool off.'

'It's where you *chose* to cool off that spelled the end of our marriage,' Lindsey stormed.

'Still trying to justify yourself?' Tim retorted. 'It doesn't matter any longer, so why can't you at least be honest? You wanted to end our marriage regardless. It wasn't working out as you'd planned, and you were afraid that sooner or later I'd return to Evebury and join the family firm.'

'That wasn't why I left, and you know it,' Lindsey stormed. 'I went because you made love to Patsy.'

'For God's sake, woman! Don't you think you over-reacted to one goddamned kiss?'

'*One kiss*? Is that what you call it?'

'What would *you* call it?'

'Adultery! Or do you expect me to believe you didn't go to bed with her the night you left me?'

Carefully Tim set down his glass on the table beside him. 'Is that what you thought?'

With equal care, Lindsey replied. 'Don't tell me you stayed at her apartment and slept on the floor! I went round there, you know.'

'The apartment is Peter's—her brother. Patsy was staying in his spare room while her own place was being redecorated. And, to set the record straight, I slept on the living-room sofa.'

Desperately Lindsey tried to grasp what she was hearing. She had believed for so long that after their quarrel Tim had rushed off to Patsy's bed that she couldn't take in that she was wrong. Yet his expression, his whole demeanour, testified to it.

What a fool she had been. And because of it, her marriage was in ruins.

'I can't prove I'm speaking the truth,' Tim went on flatly. 'And there's only one more thing I have to say on the subject. Well, two, to be precise. First, it was stupid of me to have kissed Patsy; put it down to bruised ego and anger with you. I'm not giving that as an excuse so much as a reason. And secondly, I've never made love to her in my life.'

'I—I believe you.'

'But at the time you thought the worst of me, didn't you?'

'Yes. I knew you weren't happy with me, and I thought——'

'I was extremely happy with *you*,' he corrected her. 'What I didn't like was the life you'd mapped out for me.'

Lindsey ignored this, anxious to remind him of something equally as important. 'Why didn't you make any protest when I told you I was going to New York?'

'I assumed you found our marriage a hindrance to your career. That's why I thought you'd magnified our quarrel out of all proportion—so that it gave you an excuse to leave me.' He flung out his hands. 'Seems we were both wrong.'

Lindsey was bereft of words. The truth had come too late. Tim was going to marry Francesca, making it pointless to admit that she herself still loved him.

'Pity we said our goodbyes on the telephone,' she whispered eventually. 'If we had spoken face to face we might have...' Her voice died away and she longed to run to her room and hide. But her legs wouldn't carry her that far. In their present jelly-like state she'd be lucky if they took her to the edge of the carpet.

'Odd to think we parted for nothing,' Tim mused.

'Yes. But at least you benefited from it. Look where you are today. You have a great career and a highly suitable second marriage in the offing.'

'The same could be said of you.'

Lindsey knew he was thinking of Robert and was hard put to it not to confess she was by no means sure she was going to marry him. Remembering the heartache she had endured, she could not understand why Tim— if he had loved her when she had left him—had made no attempt to get her back. Granted he had believed she wanted the separation, but his acceptance of it showed a passivity that precluded any deep feelings.

'I don't think your love was very strong.' She spoke without inflexion. 'You knew where to find me in New York, yet you made no attempt to see me.'

'I might have if my father hadn't been ill. But it was four weeks before he was off the danger list and by then I saw our situation more rationally. I didn't know you thought I'd gone to bed with Patsy, and thinking over your behaviour, it seemed to me that you felt we were——'

'Better off apart?' Lindsey finished for him.

'You must have thought so too,' Tim submitted. 'Telephones work both ways, you know. When I didn't hear from you, I took it to mean you were glad to be rid of me. Your choice for husband number two has proved me right.'

'What you mean is that Robert is more my sort of person? The same deprived background, and no rich Daddy to help us!'

'What *I* meant,' Tim emphasised the personal pronoun, 'was that you both had the determination to surmount a difficult childhood; the ability to work hard and make sacrifices in order to achieve your goals; the charisma to charm your friends and flail your enemies.'

Lindsey stared at Tim helplessly, the ground cut from under her. 'You honestly see me like that?' she asked huskily.

'I always have. And I said it too. Many times. But you didn't take it on board. You were too busy shoring up your insecurity and cutting everyone else down to size.'

She winced. How cruel he was. But how accurate.

'Yet you loved me once,' she said tremulously. 'That doesn't say much for your judgement.'

'Maybe. But it says a hell of a lot for my clairvoyance! Take a look at the person you are today, Lindsey! Secure in your confidence; accepting your success with genuine humbleness, and a double dose of charisma with not a flail in sight!'

Colour bloomed in her cheeks, but before she could speak the telephone rang, and Tim went to the hall to answer it.

'Lawson for you,' he informed her, returning.

Silently scourging Robert for his timing, Lindsey went outside and lifted the receiver.

'Sorry I was in such a lousy mood the other day,' Robert apologised. 'Will you forgive me?'

'Yes.'

'Any chance of my seeing you tonight?'

'No.'

'Tomorrow, then? Meet me for lunch, darling?'

'I can't.'

'Why so monosyllabic?' he asked irritably. 'I suppose Ramsden is around?'

'Yes.'

'What's with you, for God's sake! You're doing him a favour, yet you're the one who's pussyfooting around. If we want to meet, he has no right to object so long as no one sees us. I wish like hell you'd never gone back to him.'

'I'll say amen to that!'

'Great!' Robert didn't hide his elation. 'Any chance of you changing your mind about tomorrow? I'll bring a picnic hamper to the apartment.'

'Very well. I'll be there at one. But I can't stay long.'

'Just long enough for me to hold you.'

With trembling hands Lindsey set down the telephone and turned to see Tim at the threshold of the sitting-room.

'Sorry about the call,' she apologised.

'You have no reason to be. My phone isn't tapped, as far as I know, so Carlo Malvini won't find out!'

She half smiled. 'Shall we go in to dinner or do you want to shower and change first?'

'Shower first,' he agreed, moving to the stairs. 'But I won't join you for dinner if you don't mind? I've a stack of work to do, and I've told Mrs Parker I'll have a tray in my study.'

He was on the first step when Lindsey spoke.

'Would you like me to keep out of your way whenever you're home?' she asked abruptly.

'That isn't necessary. I honestly do have papers to go over tonight, and I—well, I'm not in the mood for company.'

'Because Francesca's gone?'

'One could put it that way.'

'How would *you* put it?'

'I already have. Papers to go over!'

Counting to ten, Lindsey walked slowly into the dining-room and closed the door behind her.

CHAPTER FIFTEEN

LINDSEY awoke next morning with a nagging sense of unease, then remembered she was having lunch with Robert. If only she hadn't agreed to their meeting at the apartment. If he tried to make love to her...

Pushing aside the thought as she pushed away the duvet, she washed her face, smoothed her hair, and went down to breakfast.

Tim had already left, but there was a brief note from him saying he wished to leave for Evebury at five.

The prospect filled her with dismay. The friendliest of in-laws could not feel any warmth towards a girl who had walked out on their adored son because—as they thought—she considered her career more important than her marriage; and since Mrs Ramsden had disliked her anyway, their anger was likely to have been stronger. But now that Tim knew the real reason she had left him, she hoped he would tell his parents the truth. She didn't see why she should appear in a bad light for nothing.

Too restless to remain in the house, she went early to the rented apartment. She had no intention of living there when she left Tim, and packed all the books and other bits and pieces she had left there in a case, and carried it out to her car.

She had just returned to the apartment and taken off her coat when Robert arrived, replete with hamper and wine. Compared with Tim, he looked thick-set and ruddy-skinned, though he was a handsome man none the less. Handsome, intelligent, and dynamic. Yet she felt no spark when she saw him, experienced no lightening of the heart. He wasn't the man for her and no amount of pretending was going to make it so.

With absolute certainty she knew it was impossible
for her to marry him.

Setting down the hamper and wine, he went to pull
her close, but she made herself busy searching out
glasses, hoping he didn't realise she was evading him.

In a flurry of indecision she wondered whether to tell
him now or wait. But wait for what? To see if it was
possible to make Tim fall in love with her again? Even
if he didn't, marrying Robert was out of the question.

Yet Tim wasn't completely immune to her, regardless
of what he said about Francesca. There was something
in his eyes when he regarded her, a tension in his body
when she came near him, that told her he still desired
her. But though the sexual chemistry between them was
still strong, it was worthless without love. Yet, worthless
or not, if it was offered to her temporarily, she would
take it.

'I was delighted when you agreed to come here to meet
me,' Robert declared, handing her a glass of wine. 'With
other women I've always been in control, but with you
it's the other way round.'

'I'm not in control,' Lindsey protested, glad her
thoughts weren't visible. 'I'm buffeted by all kinds of
emotions and I don't know where I'm at.'

'That's because you think too much.' His wide mouth
curved in a smile. 'Go with the flow!'

If I did, Lindsey thought, I'd flow into Tim's arms
and damn the consequences. Knowing she dared not say
this, she hurriedly changed to a relatively safe subject.
'Any idea how long this takeover battle will last?'

'Your husband's in a better position to know that!'

'You're like two little boys fighting over the same
bone.'

'It's a bone that means more to me than to him,'
Robert said bitterly. 'If I lose this battle, *I'll* end up being
taken over too. That's why I'm prepared to fight for
Malvini's, no matter how long it takes.'

Lindsey felt a surge of hope. The battle could last for months. Why, anything might happen by then! Francesca could fall out of love, or might get tired of waiting. What a hope! Yet hope was all she had to sustain her.

'Does it worry you?' Robert asked.

'Worry me?' she echoed, not comprehending.

'Continuing your pretence of being happily married. Or aren't you pretending?'

Lindsey busied herself laying out the food from the hamper: French liver pâté, chicken salad, and fresh raspberries with cream. 'Tim loves another woman. I told you that weeks ago.'

'I know. None the less I have the impression that living under the same roof has set you thinking of the happy times you had with him, and forgetting the bad.'

Such perception deserved honesty, and she gave it to him. 'I suppose you're right. That's why I'm not yet ready to think of marrying someone else. I need time to decide what to do with my life.'

'You don't need time,' Robert maintained forcefully, 'so much as a good memory. In all the years you and Ramsden were apart, he didn't try to see you or contact you, and when you re-entered his life what did he have to say? "Come and live with me until I've won an engineering company that I want!" If you can't see he's just using you, you must be blind!' Robert reached out and caught her by the shoulders. 'Don't send me away, Lindsey. Wait till the takeover is won and you're on your own. Then give yourself a chance with me.'

Unwilling to upset him, she gave him the promise he wanted, and by the time they parted a couple of hours later he was in a good mood.

Pity she couldn't say the same for herself. She felt she had been walking on eggshells, and her tension headache proved it.

Arriving home, she saw Tim's car parked outside the garage and, entering the house, found him in the hall.

'I'm not late, am I?' she asked. 'You said five.'

'I know. But unless you've anything specific to do I'd like to leave as soon as possible.'

'I'll be packed in ten minutes.'

'We might be staying for longer than a weekend.'

Halfway up the stairs, she stopped and turned. 'How come?'

'The fight is hotting up.'

'Shouldn't you be staying in London, then?'

He smiled. 'Sometimes it's advantageous to enjoy a few weeks' relaxation in one's country home.'

'In other words you want Robert to think you're so confident of winning that you can take a holiday.'

'Not Lawson,' Tim said. 'Signor Malvini.'

'How cunning you businessmen are!'

'Unlike the angelic executives who run TV stations?'

Flinging him a rueful smile, Lindsey went to her room. She had been nervous enough about spending the weekend with her in-laws, and the prospect of its being several weeks filled her with dismay. But at least she wasn't the gauche young girl of the past, and if Mrs Ramsden made any cutting remarks to her she'd have them returned tenfold!

Her case packed, she rang for Parker to carry it downstairs, and followed him to the car, surprised to see Tim at the wheel.

Reluctantly she got in beside him. It was only the second occasion she had been alone in a car with him, and she felt tense and self-conscious. She fastened her safety-belt and he eased the car down the road and into the busy stream of traffic. He was an excellent driver, but then he had always been confident at the wheel—a confidence that had been missing from their marriage.

She was musing over this when a snuffling noise caught her ear, and, glancing round, she saw the cat basket on the rear seat.

'You've brought Nuisance!'

'Aren't you pleased?'

'Of course.' Turning, she hoisted the basket on to her lap and gingerly lifted the lid. A rough little tongue instantly licked her finger, and she stroked the furry body before closing the lid. Immediately an ear-splitting miaow filled the car.

'Why don't you let him out?' Tim asked, raising his voice above the caterwauling.

'I thought you'd object.'

'Not if he behaves himself. He's an amusing little blighter.'

'It never occurred to me you'd want to bring him,' Lindsey confessed, happily opening the lid.

The kitten leapt out and curled up next to her, and momentarily Tim stroked the soft little body. 'He'll enjoy the countryside. There are so many field mice around, he'll think he's in paradise!'

Lindsey laughed. 'He'll hate returning to London.'

'He'll hate your apartment more. Or will you be moving in with Lawson?'

'No,' she replied abruptly.

'Sorry, I didn't mean to pry.'

Lindsey longed to admit she was not going to marry Robert, but was afraid Tim might guess the reason, and they drove several miles in silence before he spoke.

'I spoke to my parents last night and—er—put them in the picture as to the real reason you went off to New York.'

'Thank you. That should make the atmosphere easier.'

'You don't have to put on an act with me in front of them, either.'

'It isn't an effort to be friendly towards you,' she answered, turning to look at him. In profile he was like the young Tim of the past, his casual cream denims and yellow knit silk sweater enhancing this impression. 'Is it an effort for *you*?'

'It isn't easy,' he murmured. 'When I'm with you it brings back the past, and that's something I'd prefer to forget.'

The remark cut deep and her throat tightened with suppressed tears, so that it was an enormous effort for her to speak normally. 'It's the same with me,' she lied.

Nuisance chose that moment to jump on to Tim's lap, and Tim slowed the car and with one hand tried to remove him. But the kitten dug in his claws and refused to budge.

'Get him off me, will you, Lindsey?'

Leaning forward, she carefully prised the kitten off Tim's trousers, colour staining her cheeks as the tips of her fingers brushed against the hard muscle of his leg. Quickly turning away, she unceremoniously dumped Nuisance in his basket and closed the lid.

Tim grinned. 'I was expecting you to give him a cuddle first!'

'Watch it!' she retorted. 'Or I might start believing you're sentimental over an animal.'

'It's safer than waxing sentimental over a woman!'

'Have you really become as cynical as you sound? You're giving me an awful guilt complex.'

'Unnecessarily so. I'm happier this way.'

'Does Francesca know?'

He did not answer, and she let the conversation lapse and gazed unseeingly out the window.

Her nervousness increased the nearer they drew to Evebury, and when they finally came to a stop outside the beautiful stone manor house set in fifteen acres of park land, her heart was beating like a sledgehammer. Evebury Hall was smaller than she remembered it, and seemed less forbidding, though this was possibly due to the setting sun, which turned the stone a warm apricot colour.

Mr and Mrs Ramsden were waiting in the drawing-room to meet them, their manner surprisingly friendly towards Lindsey, though she noticed a perceptible tremor in the woman's hands as she motioned her to an armchair.

The years had dealt kindly with Tim's parents, and Lindsey was at a loss to understand why they seemed so different, until she realised that the difference was in herself. Tim's father, whose patrician air and clipped tones used to intimidate her, now seemed merely an older version of his handsome son and, because of it, not intimidating at all; while Tim's mother, whom she remembered as perennially elegant in Gucci brogues, expensive tweeds and cashmere, today wore trainers, a baggy plaid skirt and cotton shirt.

Mrs Ramsden, aware of Lindsey's perusal, glanced down at herself. 'I've been gardening,' she explained, 'and you arrived earlier than I expected.'

'I didn't know you gardened.'

'It's my hobby.'

'Her obsession,' her husband corrected. 'For the past twenty years we haven't bought a flower or vegetable. Do *you* have green fingers, my dear?'

'Only when it comes to arranging flowers—I haven't had the opportunity of growing any.'

'Lindsey's a cat lover,' Tim interposed.

'Heavens!' she cried, jumping to her feet, 'we left him in the car!'

'I'll fetch him,' Tim volunteered.

'How does London compare with New York?' Mrs Ramsden asked as her son disappeared, followed by his father.

'It's more relaxed.'

'Are you still working in television?'

'Not at the moment. I always have a long break in the summer.'

'That was lucky for Tim. We—my husband and I— really appreciate what you are doing for him. It can't be an easy situation for you.'

'It's easier than I thought it would be. But mainly it's boring.'

'Boring? But Tim is so——'

'Not Tim,' Lindsey grinned, unable to stop herself. 'But my doing nothing. I'm unused to being a lady of leisure, and he has a full-time daily help, and Mrs Parker to do the housekeeping and cooking.'

'I'm sure she wouldn't object if you did a meal occasionally. You're an excellent cook. We dined with you once and I was most impressed.'

Lindsey was startled, vaguely recalling the one and only occasion her in-laws had visited their apartment. How nervous she had been, conscious of its dreary location, its smallness, and the cheap furniture with not an antique in sight!

'You made roast beef and a wonderful banana soufflé,' Mrs Ramsden went on.

'Soufflés are easy.'

'Only if one has the self-confidence,' Mrs Ramsden smiled. 'But then you have a great deal of that.'

'Now, perhaps,' Lindsey admitted. 'I didn't years ago. The opposite, in fact.'

'It wasn't apparent.'

'I was a good actress.'

Before Mrs Ramsden could reply, the two men returned, Nuisance under Tim's arm, and with the Siamese as the focus of attention the atmosphere became easier.

At half-past six they all retired to change. When Lindsey had stayed here previously, she and Tim had shared his old bedroom, but now they were in two adjoining rooms, with a connecting door and the key on her side.

She heard him moving around and pictured him taking off his sweater. Was his chest still covered with thick golden hair, and was there still that faint bruised shadow in the hollow beneath his collarbone? It had always made her feel tender, and she had loved to press her lips to it as Tim played with her hair.

'Stop harking back to the past,' she ordered herself, speaking aloud to give the words greater force. 'Francesca's important to him now. Not you.'

Resolutely pushing aside the memories of her marriage, she went into the bathroom to shower.

CHAPTER SIXTEEN

REALISING she had a part to play, and determined to play it to the hilt, Lindsey dressed with great care.

Five years ago her in-laws had always dressed formally for dinner, and she was pretty sure that the easy-going ways of the Nineties hadn't altered their attitude. Boundaries of countries might change, the moon be colonised, but people like Mr and Mrs Ramsden still donned formal attire for their evening meal!

She finally settled for a violet, ankle-length satin skirt, its fullness drawing attention to her narrow waist, and a pink, long-sleeved georgette blouse, against which her hair glowed like molten fire.

Giving herself a final glance in the mirror, she left her room and stood hesitating in the corridor, not sure whether to wait for Tim. Deciding against it, she went downstairs, but there was no one about and she strolled on to the terrace.

Dusk had settled, and in its blue haze the sky almost merged with the distant hills. A cool breeze stirred the leaves and lifted the ruffles of her blouse, and she moved back into the drawing-room, enjoying the delicate tracery of leaves and ferns on the parchment-coloured Chinese wallpaper, and the soft pastels of the slightly faded damask silk armchairs.

Beyond the door was the hall and winding staircase. Tim had once told her he had loved sliding down the banisters when a child, and she pictured other children doing the same. Sturdy little boys with golden hair, and dainty girls with red ringlets. She shook her head, angry with herself for daydreaming. There'd be no red-haired children here. Only blonde and black-haired ones.

Anxious to dispel such a disturbing image, she wandered round the room, touching the delicate porcelain figurines on the carved marble mantelpiece, and a beautifully inlaid escritoire on the top of which stood a series of family photographs. There were several of Tim taken at varying ages, and she was admiring them when a footstep behind her made her turn, and she saw the man himself watching her.

In a cream mohair silk dinner-jacket, his dark gold hair gleaming from vigorous brushing, he was a romantic hero come to life. 'You should have helped yourself to a drink,' he said.

'I didn't think of it. I was busy enjoying this room. It's lovely. But then so is the whole house.'

'That's a change in your thinking. You used to say you disliked it.'

'Because it overpowered me; made me feel insignificant.'

'And it doesn't any longer?'

'No. Now I can understand why you love it.'

'I'm glad.'

She longed to say *she* could love it here too, but was afraid that admitting to this feeling might give away others she preferred to keep hidden.

'You're lucky to have Ramsden Engineering so near here,' she contented herself with saying. 'You can look after the company and stay in your home at the same time!'

Tim nodded. 'That's something I appreciate. I try to get down most weekends.'

Lindsey pictured Tim and herself strolling amid daffodils and crocuses by the lake in the spring sunshine; tramping through autumn woods, the ground rich with golden leaves, or stalking across snow covered fields beneath a crisp blue winter sky.

'Tim!' Mr Ramsden hurried in, mercifully cutting short her thoughts. 'Mr Dunford is on the line.'

Tim swung round to the door. 'I'll take the call in the library.'

'He never manages to get a weekend to himself,' his father frowned. 'Someone or other always wants to talk to him. I wish you could get him to totally relax.'

'I can't see him listening to *me*.'

'You're his wife. Surely you——' Mr Ramsden stopped abruptly, his skin turning pink with embarrassment. 'My dear, how incredibly tactless of me.'

Lindsey forced a smile to her lips. 'Not really. It just shows what a good act Tim and I are putting on.'

'Carlo Malvini is making a secret flight to London,' Tim announced walking back into the room. 'That's why Jack called me.'

'It can't be a secret if Mr Dunford knows,' Mr Ramsden remarked.

'Nothing is secret from Jack.'

'Or sacred either,' Lindsey couldn't help adding. 'I suppose he also knows why the man's coming over?'

'That's something he *hasn't* been able to ascertain—yet! But he's working on it.'

'It's my opinion that Signor Malvini is about to make a decision,' Mr Ramsden interpolated.

Tim nodded and moved closer to his father. 'I agree with you.'

His voice sank lower as the two men discussed all the implications of the flight, and as they talked Lindsey's one thought was that her days with the man she loved were numbered. For her there was never going to be an autumn in Evebury, let alone winter and spring. In a matter of weeks, days perhaps, they would part forever.

Her gaze rested on Tim. Although he had always maintained an air of calm confidence over the battle ensuing between him and Robert for control of the Italian company, now that he was in the family home with his parents he had lowered his guard, giving a glimpse of the tension he hid from the business world.

'Why does winning the Italian company mean so much to you?' she asked as his conversation with his father ceased and he went over to the tray on the sideboard.

'It would be my first major acquisition since becoming chairman.'

'Do you need to keep proving yourself? I'd have thought your track record was already good enough.'

'Lindsey has a point there,' Mr Ramsden interpolated, dry humour edging his voice. 'Or does Semperton Trust want to buy up the world?'

'Not quite,' Tim replied. 'There's one more company we want after this one, then we'll ease up on our expansion.' He handed a whiskey to his father, then sauntered across to Lindsey to give her a glass of champagne. 'You should be pleased you won't have to continue with this sham for much longer,' he murmured.

She lowered her eyes, scared he might see her love for him in them. What irony that he believed her pretence would end when they parted. That was when her real charade would begin—allowing him to believe she wanted a divorce in order to marry Robert.

The remainder of the evening was spent discussing why Carlo Malvini was coming to England, though Lindsey was only aware that every passing moment brought her nearer to her final parting from Tim.

At ten-thirty she pleaded tiredness and went to her room. But it was impossible to sleep, and for what seemed an eternity she sat in her nightgown staring out at the moonlit lawn and trying not to think of the bleakness of her future. Heavens above, she still had her career and, if Grace Chapman's enthusiasm for her was anything to go by, she could be as great a success in England as in the States. But no, staying on this side of the Atlantic was too bitter-sweet, and the greater the physical distance between herself and Tim, the better for her peace of mind.

It was close to midnight when she heard Tim moving around in his room. She envisaged him undressing, her fevered imagination following his every movement, and when there was eventually silence, her mind's eye saw him in bed, body relaxed, arms empty...

A tap at her door startled her out of her chair, and she called, 'Come in.' The door remained shut, and realising that the tapped door was not the one leading into the corridor, but the communicating one, she stepped over to unlock it.

'Sorry,' she said nervously, seeing Tim on the threshold. 'Is anything wrong?'

'That's what I was going to ask *you*! I noticed you still had the light on, and wondered if you were all right. You were rather quiet this evening.'

'I was nervous, I guess.'

'Forget it. You'll do fine.' He came further into the room, tightening the belt of his black silk dressing-gown. The tension that had buoyed him up earlier had disappeared, and he looked tired.

'What exactly am I expected to do while I'm here?' she questioned, conscious of his nearness, and mindful of the transparency of her nightgown.

'Act the loving wife and let it be known how happy you are with me. A hard act, I know, but I'm sure you will do it brilliantly.'

'I wish you weren't so bitter. I know our marriage went wrong, but neither of us was guiltless.'

'I'm not bitter. I'm saddened by it.' His eyes ranged over her, the sudden twisting of his mouth showing he was under the spell of some deep emotion. 'I loved you without reservation. You know that, don't you? You were the most beautiful girl I'd ever encountered. So vibrant, so eager to conquer the world. You were the only woman I ever asked to share my life; the only one I wanted to wake up in the morning and see in my bed.' His hand came out to caress the side of her face. 'The way I see it now,' he muttered. 'It's no use, is it, Lindsey? The chemistry is still there and I can't fight it.'

Lowering his head, he covered her mouth with his, stifling her answer. It was the kiss of a man who had held himself in check for too long; a passionate, demanding, draining kiss that sent a flame of desire shooting through her body. Her limbs grew weak and she clung to him, her nipples hardening, twin peaks of throbbing desire that set up the same fire between her thighs. She willed herself not to respond to his searching tongue, but it was a losing fight. The heavy pounding of his heart set her own beating in unison, and she gave a guttural cry as his mouth sought her breasts through the silk of her nightgown.

'I need you,' he groaned, half leading, half carrying her to the bed.

She could have resisted, or at least put up a token fight, but the touch of his hands, the taste of his mouth, the heat of his desire—which emanated from him as if it were something tangible—robbed her of all thought except one: to give herself to him.

Pliantly she allowed him to remove her flimsy covering, her body trembling as he feasted his eyes on her before slowly moving his hands over the soft swell of her stomach, the curve of her breasts, the smooth line of her shoulders. His dressing-gown had slipped off and she gloried in the magnificent nakedness of his firm, masculine flesh, revelled in the strength and size of him, knowing that soon she would make him part of her.

'My red-haired witch,' he whispered, sliding down until his body masked hers. 'I was never able to resist you.'

Her lips parted beneath his, and his tongue, hot and moist, explored the inner recesses of her mouth before charting every inch of her. Her mind became a total blank, receptive only to Tim's touch, to his tongue and fingertips trailing a path of ecstasy all over her body.

'You're glorious,' he said, his voice tormented by desire as he poised above her.

Yet he made no attempt to appease his appetite, though her body arched beneath as she pulled him closer and pressed her heated wetness upon his throbbing arousal.

He moved back, but as she cried out her loss his fingers twined in the damp hair of her mound, then found the soft inner lips, rubbing them lightly until they unfolded and he could touch the small, tumescent nub, the centre core, the heart of her being. She writhed in a torment of passion, aching to enclose him, to make his life-force her own.

The years since they had last made love evaporated; it was as if they had never parted, so familiar was his touch, so complete their knowledge of each other's bodies. This was not lovemaking between young sweethearts; this was the driving passion of experienced lovers, moved by the same tide, anticipating the same final flood of fulfilment.

With a lithe movement she twisted away from him, and he turned upon his back to see her. Instantly she came down on him, her legs parted, her body open to take him in. His shaft went deep inside her and she expanded to absorb him fully, then tightened her muscles to hold him there.

He groaned deep in his throat, his hands gripping her buttocks as she rode him. Subtly, slowly, he took command, and new sensations washed over her as he plunged deeper, rock-hard yet smooth as silk. Her heart pounded and she met him thrust for thrust until his body reared up and, with a racking cry, he climaxed inside her, his fiery fluid sending her spiralling into a bone-melting ecstasy that left her mindless.

Exhausted, she lay upon him like a limp doll, and tenderly he clasped his arms around her and swung her gently on to her side, fitting her into the curves of his body, like a glove on a hand.

I'm home again, she thought. This is where I belong. In the arms of the man I love. If only she could tell him she longed to be his wife forever, but common sense interceded and kept her silent.

It was impossible for her to talk of love when he had only talked of chemistry. What they had just shared meant physical relief for him, not a communion of spirit, and for her to bare her soul to him would do nothing other than embarrass him.

Curled against him, her head nestling in the soft niche between his neck and shoulder, she listened to the soft sound of his breathing and the quickened beat of his heart. As always after they had made love, she was filled with delicious contentment, unwilling to move and spill the seed he had gushed into her.

I want his baby. The thought, lighter than a feather's fall, seeped into her consciousness, gaining force with every passing millisecond, until it took her over completely. Could she? Dared she?

She had taken the Pill for years to regulate her monthly cycle, but if she stopped taking it...

She tilted her head the better to see Tim's face. The warmth of passion still coloured his skin, and though faint lines fanned his eyes and marked the sides of his mouth, all tension had gone. Before the year was out, Francesca would be his wife, but for the next three weeks he could be hers, and if the result was a child, a part of him for her to cherish...

Trembling, she weighed up the advantages and disadvantages. At least she wouldn't be an unmarried mother because the baby would be conceived in wedlock, though no one would know of it, of course. It would be her secret, as would the father's name. It also meant returning to live permanently in America, for only there, completely out of Tim's life, would her secret be safe.

Her thoughts flew further into the future, and she was no longer so sanguine. A baby didn't ask questions, but a child might, and a teenager certainly would. And did she have the right to deny her child its father? Especially when the father was someone like Tim?

Regretfully she abandoned the idea. It was a wonderful pipe-dream, but her own particular code—forged by years in an orphanage—didn't allow her to make it a reality.

For the moment Tim was hers. But only Tim; not his children.

She mustn't think of the past and the regrets it conjured up; nor of the future and what might have been. She must think only of what *was*, and enjoy every second of it, for today's pleasures were going to be the wonderful memories of tomorrow and tomorrow and tomorrow.

CHAPTER SEVENTEEN

EARLY morning sunlight, seeping in through the half drawn curtains, awakened Lindsey from a dreamless slumber and, half opening her eyes, she reached for Tim.

He wasn't there. Fully awake now, she sat up and looked around. The bedroom was empty, the pillow beside her smooth as though no blond head had rested there. Had it all been a dream? A desire so desperately longed for that it had been conjured up by an imagination gone mad?

Jumping out of bed, she saw a slither of green satin on the carpet. Her nightgown! Slipping it on, she padded across to the mirror. No crazy woman looked back at her; just the face she saw every morning. Yet not quite. Peering closer, she stared at the small love bite at the base of her neck, where Tim had kissed her.

Enveloped by memories that brought colour to her skin, she donned a matching dressing-gown, ran a brush through her hair, and went in search of him.

Not yet six, it was too early for any of the staff to be up, and she found him in the kitchen, frowning with absorption as he measured coffee into an electric percolator and switched it on. His hair was still slightly damp from his shower and curled upon his neck, instead of lying smoothly. It made him appear younger and vulnerable, and she longed to run her hands over his head and put her arms around his body.

She moved towards him, then stopped, uncertain how he would react. 'Good morning, Tim, you're awake early.'

He swung round. 'So are you.' He met her eyes briefly, then lowered his head. 'Care for a cup of coffee?'

'Absolutely. It smells delicious.' Why were they discussing coffee when they should be talking about last night? she wondered. And why wasn't he looking at her? Was he worried that she thought he had seduced her? 'Tim, about last night—I——'

'You don't know how bitterly I regret it,' he cut in. 'I deserve every name you care to call me.'

'I'm not angry.'

'That makes me feel worse! I used you, Lindsey. When I walked into your room and saw you in that green nightgown it brought back memories and—well, I lost control. It's never happened to me before, and I give you my word it won't happen again.' He slammed down his hand so hard on the counter top that the percolator jumped. 'I behaved like a crazed animal.'

An animal because he had made love to her? But Tim wasn't talking about love. All he had felt was lust, and he had just made that painfully clear. That was why he was angry with himself: because he had given in to his baser emotions.

'Can you forgive me?' he begged.

She stared at the stranger in front of her. For that was what he was: a stranger she loved. Was he so insensitive that he was unaware of the depth of her response to him? The passion with which she had reciprocated his touch, his thrusting urgency? Or did he believe that, like himself, lust had caused her orgasm?

'There's nothing to forgive,' she said huskily.

'You mean that?'

'Yes.'

And she did. He hadn't entered her room with the set purpose of seducing her. Nor had it been triggered by sight of her green nightgown, identical in colour to the one she had worn when they had made love before her fateful Paris trip. No, regardless of what he believed, the truth was that he had subconsciously sensed the signals she had given out.

So if anyone was to blame, it was she. He had asked her to delay the divorce and return to him solely to protect his business ambitions. But she, loving him, had read into it what she wished to believe. And wishing didn't make true.

'Please don't blame yourself,' she reiterated. 'Sex was always good between us, and being thrown together as we are—with you away from Francesca, and me away from Robert—well, it was on the cards that we might——' About to say 'make love', she hastily let the rest of her sentence fade, and when she spoke again her tone was determinedly bright. 'I suggest we forget the whole thing and concentrate on the reason we are temporarily together.'

A faint smile curved Tim's mouth and he finally met her eyes. 'You were always able to get to the heart of the matter, weren't you?'

'Some things never change.' Her nonchalant shrug as she poured herself a cup of coffee was a masterpiece of acting. 'Take a pew and I'll fix you breakfast. Do you still have your daily bacon and eggs, sunny side up?'

'I now only indulge myself on Saturday and Sunday. During the week it's toast and fruit juice.'

'Well, it's Saturday today...'

'Then I'll indulge!'

Opening the refrigerator, she took out the ingredients she required, glad she could keep her face turned away from his as she prepared the food.

'You always cooked a mean breakfast,' Tim complimented her as she deftly placed the sizzling eggs on warmed plates, together with slices of crisp-edged bacon. 'This, and soufflés, were what you excelled in.'

'It was pretty well the extent of my repertoire in those days!' she reminded him, her emotions firmly under control. 'Your mother still doesn't know that. She thinks my brilliant soufflés are just one sign of my prowess as a chef!'

'I promise she won't learn the truth from me,' Tim grinned, 'so rest easy!'

'I will anyway. I'll have you know you're looking at a woman with a cookery diploma. During my second year in New York, cookery classes were part of the ethnic scene!'

'I don't see you as a *hausfrau*.'

'Not a permanent one,' she agreed. 'But it's enjoyable to do it occasionally.'

'Sounds as if you and Lawson are planning a family?'

The question, casually uttered, almost shattered her control, and hurriedly she collected their empty plates and stacked them in the sink. 'Why should you find that surprising?' she asked from a safe distance.

'I had you placed as a serious career woman.'

'I am. But that doesn't preclude having a family. I've always planned on having one. You know that.'

'Times change and so do people.'

'*I* haven't—at least not in that respect.' Flagellating herself, she threw his question back at him. 'What about you? Do you and Francesca envisage the patter of tiny feet?'

'We haven't discussed it. But I like children, and Francesca has two sisters and three brothers, so I suppose there's your answer.'

Blindly Lindsey turned back to the sink and fiddled with the dishes.

'Leave them,' Tim said behind her.

The entry of a maid precluded further conversation and, murmuring that she was going to shower, Lindsey returned to her room.

If only she could leave this house; leave Tim and never see him again. But she had promised to stay with him for as long as necessary, and she wouldn't go back on her word. Yet unless she took a hold of herself she'd end up a nervous wreck.

After a couple of sleepless nights, she tried to tire herself by ruthlessly tramping the countryside during the

day, and swimming countless lengths in the indoor pool
her father-in-law had had installed after his heart attack.
But nothing helped, and alone in her room at night her
physical longing for Tim would overwhelm her, and it
was all she could do not to go in to him and beg him to
make love to her. For almost five years she had shunned
intimacy, but, having experienced his lovemaking again,
her body craved for more.

Oddly enough, she had no sense of guilt where Robert
was concerned, probably because she had known for
weeks that she could never marry him. Tim, of course,
loving Francesca, must be racked by remorse, and no
doubt wished he could turn back the clock.

Luckily she saw little of him, for he spent the better
part of each day at Ramsden Engineering with Jack
Dunford, who returned with him each evening. After
dinner they would retire to the library, and she couldn't
help wondering if Tim genuinely had work to occupy
him or felt so guilty for having gone to bed with her that
he had to keep out of her way? If this was the case,
perhaps he wouldn't object if she suggested she return
to London. Even a few days away from him would be
a welcome relief from the torment of being near him.

'Out of the question,' he stated when she mentioned
it.

His blunt refusal angered her. 'Why? Even genuinely
happily couples don't necessarily live in each other's
pockets.'

'I agree. But *we* have been apart for nearly five years,
and since this is the first time we've been at Evebury
together in all that time, it's hardly likely you'd wish to
go tearing back to London.'

'You talk as if Signor Malvini is having us watched!'

'He is,' said Jack Dunford, coming into the room and
hearing Lindsey's last remark. 'It's true,' he added,
seeing her disbelief. 'He's having Robert Lawson watched
too.'

'Robert? Does he know?'

'Thinking of telling him?' came the acid reply, and Lindsey flushed to the roots of her hair.

'That comment is uncalled for, Jack,' Tim said quietly.

'Sorry,' the man mumbled, and strode out.

'He's very loyal to me,' Tim explained, by way of another apology. 'But to answer your question, Lawson attended service at his local church on Sunday—the first time in years apparently—so it would seem he *does* know!'

Although still ruffled by Jack's less than tactful comment to her, Lindsey couldn't help smiling.

'Signor Malvini must be a very obsessive person,' she remarked a moment later. 'I mean, one can't force one's standards on to others.'

'He isn't trying to. He simply wants to ensure that whoever runs his company thinks the way he does.'

'If it's between you and Robert,' Lindsey said tartly, moving to the door, 'he's a loser whoever he chooses! You're both putting on an act.' Not waiting for his response, she walked out and closed the door behind her.

In the hall, she paused. Talking of Robert had reminded her that she had not spoken to him for far too long, and feeling remiss, she decided to call him. Going into the library and intentionally leaving the door open—to show Jack and Tim she had nothing to hide—she dialled Robert's number.

'It's a tonic to hear your voice,' he said when he came on the line. 'I hope you're bored living in the country!'

'I hate to admit it, but I love it.' What she didn't love was being in the country with Tim, but that was something she dared not admit to Robert.

'I miss you like hell!' he grumbled. 'Any chance of you slipping off for a day? I'll meet you anywhere you name.'

'It's impossible.'

She heard a step behind her, and glancing round saw Tim. Obviously guessing to whom she was talking, he gave her an easy smile and backed out.

'I must go,' she muttered into the receiver.

'Not until we set a date,' came the firm answer. 'The day after this takeover ends, we'll meet at my apartment for dinner.'

Long after the call had ended, she remained beside the telephone, deeply regretting that she couldn't have been honest with him today, yet knowing it would have been wrong to cause him emotional pain while he was in the midst of a business battle.

As she walked back into the hall, Tim came out of the drawing-room.

'Finished your call?'

'Yes. You needn't have left me alone. I wasn't discussing anything private with Robert.'

'I thought you might be discussing sweet nothings.' His mouth curved upwards. 'I noted you left the door open.'

'Good.'

'It wasn't necessary, though. I'd trust you in every respect, Lindsey.'

The unexpected compliment brought tears to her eyes, and she hastily turned to go upstairs before he saw them. She was at the top when he called her name, and she swung round.

'I have a directors' meeting this evening in London,' he said, 'and won't be back till late.'

'You're coming back tonight?' She was surprised.

'By helicopter. So I'll see you when you wake up tomorrow—darling.'

This last sentence was said for the benefit of the housekeeper, who chose that moment to come into the hall, and Lindsey echoed the endearment and hurried to her room.

She dined with her in-laws, and to all intents and purposes they could have passed for a normal family, with Mrs Ramsden chatting about the house, and Mr Ramsden proudly regaling her with stories of the many successes his son had notched up since being brought into Semperton Trust.

It was midnight before she was in bed, but though tired she could not sleep. The wind whistled in the trees and she wondered if Tim was in the boardroom or in the air. But if it was too windy a helicopter didn't fly, did it? What was the risk element? Her hands grew clammy and she chided herself for letting her imagination run riot. Tim wasn't a fool. He wouldn't fly if the weather was wrong.

Sleepless, she lay awake in the dark, counting the passing of time, and it was well after two when she heard him return.

Ears straining, she listened to the faint sounds coming from his room, and long after there was silence she still found herself staring at the door that divided her room from Tim's. She longed for him so much that every nerve-end seemed to be tingling. How was she going to get through her life after they parted?

A low moan escaped her, and without being aware of it she found herself in his room. Hastily she went to draw back, horrified at what he would say if he saw her here.

But that was something she didn't have to fear, for he was fast asleep!

Breathing a sigh of relief, she tiptoed over to his bed and stared down at him. Unconscious, he looked different. There were still lines of tension grooving either side of his mouth, but they were not as heavily marked, and his forehead was completely smooth and serene. Because he was lying on his back, his thick hair fell away from his brow, the blondest strands that normally fell forward now visible among the darker hair. Resisting

the urge to smooth it back in case it awakened him,
Lindsey bent lower and breathed in the warmth and scent
of him.

Oh, God, how she loved this man! Tears pouring down
her cheeks, she stumbled back into her room and closed
the door.

CHAPTER EIGHTEEN

TIM had changed. Lindsey had noticed it the day after his trip to London, and now, two days later, she was certain of it.

Normally urbane and upbeat, he was a man who had always worn his worries lightly, due in no small measure to his belief that life itself was more important than anything else. It was a philosophy that had often irritated her in the past, smacking as it did of a Dr Pangloss attitude, but it was so inherent a part of him that she had never even tried to argue him out of it.

She had been intrigued to find that his success in the business world had not altered his philosophy. Indeed, from a few things Jack had let drop, it appeared to have contributed to his success.

'It enables him to keep his cool when everyone around him is going berserk,' Jack had explained. 'And the dicier the situation, the icier he becomes.'

'Is that always an advantage?'

'Yes. Logic thrives best in a cold temperature!'

Lindsey thought of this now, and wondered what chance Tim was gearing himself up to take; for that he was contemplating something dangerous was obvious to her. Why else had he become so detached and frozen in demeanour?

She had her answer the following day, when she came down to find him at the front door, grey-suited, dark blond hair brushed as flat as it would go, leather weekend case in hand.

'Where are you off to?' she asked involuntarily, and was instantly mortified. 'Sorry, it's none of my business.'

An eyebrow lifted in acknowledgement of her apology. 'I should be back tomorrow.'

Only as he went down the steps to his car did she realise he had not in fact answered her question, though when she heard the throb of the helicopter's engines a few moments later she knew that wherever Tim was off to, it wasn't close at hand.

'Looks as if we're a threesome again,' Mr Ramsden remarked as Lindsey joined her in-laws for pre dinner drinks that evening. 'Any idea where Tim has gone?'

'Afraid not.'

'It's probably something to do with this bid,' Mrs Ramsden said. 'Tim's been like a cat on a hot tin roof the past couple of days.'

'Nonsense,' her husband snorted. 'He's been extraordinarily calm.'

'That's what I mean!'

'But you said——'

'I know what I said. Now pour Lindsey her drink and let us talk of *anything* except business.'

The knowledge that Mr Ramsden didn't know where his son had gone surprised Lindsey, for since being at Evebury she had been struck by the way Tim strove to keep his father in the picture about everything concerning the bid. Could the reason for his absence be a private one? Various possibilities entered her mind, and as her curiosity grew, so did her determination to find out if she was right.

At ten o'clock, pleading a headache, she went to her room and called the security office at the headquarters of Semperton Trust. Mindful that her request would only be granted if she pulled rank, she reluctantly did.

'This is Mr Timothy Ramsden's wife,' she drawled. 'My husband used the helicopter this morning and I'd like to contact the pilot.'

Within moments she was dialling the mobile telephone number of Harry Langers.

'Langers speaking,' a gruff voice responded on the fifth ring.

'It's Mrs Ramsden. I believe you flew my husband this morning?'

'Yes, ma'am.'

'Well, I'm arranging a surprise party for him and I wonder if you can tell me exactly when he's due back from—was it Paris this time? He makes so many trips I get confused!'

'Me too,' the man chuckled. 'But it's Venice.'

Her heart lurched. Venice. The most romantic city in the world. What better place to have a tryst with Francesca?

'H-how silly of me to forget,' she managed to say.

'He wasn't certain what flight he'd be catching,' the pilot added, 'but he said he'll let me know. I can call you as soon as I hear from him.'

'No, don't bother, thanks. I—I'll arrange the dinner for nine-thirty. But please don't mention that I spoke to you. As I said, it's a surprise.'

'I've forgotten it already.'

Dropping the receiver on to its cradle, Lindsey sank down on the bed. The reason for Tim's withdrawn manner these past two days was now clear. It had nothing to do with the bid and everything to do with his love for the Italian girl. A love so strong that it had made him act with uncharacteristic indiscretion. Jack would be furious if he knew. And rightly so, for if Signor Malvini's spies had found out about this trip Semperton could kiss their bid goodbye.

She jumped to her feet. And Tim could kiss *her* goodbye! In the face of his stupid behaviour she was damned if she'd go on pretending to be his loving wife. But before she went, she'd tell him what she thought of him. Misery swamped her; not only because Tim's action had confirmed how deep his feelings were for Francesca, but because he had allowed them to jeopardise the company of which he was chairman.

Next day she was so on edge that, afraid Mrs Ramsden would notice her agitation, she went into the local market town, ostensibly to buy some walking shoes.

'I'll probably have lunch out too, and go to the cinema,' she said. 'They're showing a film I want to see.'

In the event she had no patience to sit through a film, and was home in the early afternoon. She went upstairs to put away her few parcels, thinking all the while of Tim, and whether he had left Venice or had decided to extend his stay with Francesca? After all, in for a penny, in for a pound. And he was the one who had made a fuss about her seeing Robert! So intent was she on fighting her anger and jealousy that she was startled by a rap on her door, and hastily composed her features.

'Come in,' she called, and expecting one of the maids, was astonished to see the man she had just been mentally maligning.

'Not disturbing you, am I?' Tim enquired.

What a laugh that was! Just the mere sight of him set her heart thumping and her body trembling.

'Not at all,' she said aloud. 'Did you have an enjoyable trip?'

'Enjoyable was hardly the word.'

'How would you describe it then?' she asked, swallowing words like passionate, ardent, erotic.

'Nerve-racking,' he said.

'*Nerve-racking*?'

Closing the door, he came further into the room. He looked older, and she wasn't sure if it was because of the dark shadows beneath his eyes or because his expression was unusually resolute.

'Deciding what I had to do was difficult enough,' he explained, 'but having to tell it to my board of directors... That was hardest of all.'

The comb clattered from Lindsey's hand. 'You *told* them?'

'Naturally. I also handed them my letter of resignation. It won't be made public until Lawson announces that he's won the takeover bid, but——'

'Tim, stop! I don't know what you're talking about.'

'My going to see Carlo Malvini.'

'You went to Italy to——'

'To see him—yes. At his home in Venice.'

'I see.' Words failed her and she sent up a grateful prayer that she had warned Harry Langers to say nothing of their conversation.

Watching her, Tim frowned. 'I thought you knew where I was going?'

'No. I asked you but you didn't answer me.' She frowned. 'Why did you want to see him?'

'To tell him our reconciliation was a sham.'

Suddenly everything Tim had told her a moment ago fell into place. 'So that's why you returned to London and resigned from Semperton Trust?'

'I felt I had no choice. Though, strangely enough, three-quarters of the board wanted me to stay on, which goes to show that ethics aren't entirely dead in the City!' His eyes narrowed as he became aware of her silence. 'I suppose you think I was crazy to see Malvini?'

'Surprised is nearer the mark,' she admitted. 'But I still don't understand why.'

Tim wandered over to the window and stared out at the land sloping away into the distance. 'Because of this,' he said, gesturing to the beautiful view and the house. 'Because I grew up learning what it means to be part of a heritage, to bear a name to be proud of. Staying here these past weeks made me realise I didn't want to win a battle dishonourably.'

'What was Signor Malvini's reaction?'

'He thanked me politely, then changed the subject. We discussed world affairs until I left for the airport.'

'Does Jack know where you went? He must be livid.'

'That's the understatement of the year. Right now he's trying to get me to withdraw my resignation.'

'I think he's right. OK, so you've lost this bid, but you might have lost it anyway.'

'But I *chose* to lose it.'

'And the majority of your board understand why and want you to stay on! You *must* take back your resignation.'

'I don't feel I can.'

Tim loosened his tie and undid the top button of his shirt. In that respect he hadn't changed, Lindsey thought with tenderness. Whenever emotionally fraught, he could not bear anything constricting round his neck.

'Well, aren't you going to say it?' he asked with a faint smile.

'Say what?'

'That I carry honour to extreme.'

She shook her head. 'I'm glad you do. I—I'm proud of it.'

'Thank you.' He moved towards the dividing door. 'It means you're free to go, of course. Our charade is over.'

The words were like a knife in her solar plexus and it was all she could do to hide her pain.

'I really am grateful for the effort you made,' he added. 'You acted as if you were really my wife.'

As if you were really my wife. This was twisting the knife, and it took a superhuman effort not to cry out.

'I've never done things by half,' she managed to say, turning back to the dressing table and averting her head as if she were searching for something. 'I'll leave in the morning.'

'In that case we can go together.'

'Thanks, but I don't go a bundle on helicopters.'

'I'm driving back.' Humour edged his voice.

'Then I'll accept your offer.'

The door closed quietly, and only then did she lower her head in her hands and pray for the strength to act normally for the next twelve hours.

This meant putting in an appearance for afternoon tea, which she had made a habit of taking with Mrs Ramsden since coming here to stay, and as she went downstairs she heard Jack Dunford's angry voice coming from the library, followed by Mr Ramsden's quieter one.

'Do you think Tim was right?' her mother-in-law asked as she handed Lindsey a cup of tea.

'It's what he thinks that matters.'

'I still think he was foolish to give up the chairmanship when so many of the directors want him to stay. If he leaves, his career is finished.'

'Plenty of other companies will want him,' Lindsey assured her.

'But none is as important as Semperton Trust. If only he——'

She stopped as the door was flung open and Tim strode in, white faced, his father and Jack Dunford hard on his heels.

'It's over!' Tim said. 'Signor Malvini called a Press conference a quarter of an hour ago.'

'Oh Tim, I'm so sorry,' his mother whispered, and dabbed at her eyes.

'There's no need to be,' he admonished, crossing to her side and resting his hand on her shoulder. 'Malvini has accepted *our* bid.'

'He has? Why, that's wonderful! Now you must take back your resignation.'

'It won't be necessary.'

'Of course it's necessary. How can you be so obstinate?'

'You've got it wrong, Mrs Ramsden,' Jack Dunford intervened with a smile. 'What Tim means is that it isn't necessary because of the statement Carlo Malvini made to the Press. In effect, he said he had accepted the bid from Semperton because he had every confidence in the integrity of its chairman.' The smile widened. 'And I can assure you that, after such a comment, the board of directors will make sure Tim's their chairman for life!'

Lindsey's heart swelled with pride. No matter that Tim was no longer hers, or that his future would be spent with another woman. What counted was that he had fought a battle cleanly and won it without sacrificing his honour.

It was midnight before she got to bed, family celebrations having been interrupted by calls from the financial Press and various television and radio stations.

Only when alone in her room did she think of Robert and wish she had had the forethought to telephone him earlier. Yet, conscious of the terrible blow he had suffered, and, guiltily aware that what she had to say to him tomorrow would add to his unhappiness, she put in a call to him. If the telephone wasn't answered at the second ring she'd hang up.

'Lawson speaking,' came his deep voice.

'It's Lindsey. I didn't wake you, did I?'

'Hardly. I suppose you're calling to commiserate?'

'Yes. I'm so sorry, Robert.'

'You sound as if you mean it.'

'I do. I wish you had both been able to win.'

'Trust a woman to wish for the impossible,' he said with a dry laugh. 'But thanks for your sympathy, though I don't need it. I've already made new plans.'

'I'm glad.'

'Ramsden won't be. I'm selling out to an American company. I told you I wouldn't let him take *me* over.'

Anxious to avoid an argument, she said quickly, 'Am I still seeing you tomorrow evening?'

'Tonight,' he corrected. 'It's already past twelve.'

'So it is. Eight o'clock at my place.'

'I'm counting the hours,' he said throatily.

Putting down the receiver, she stared at it bleakly. It wasn't going to be easy to break with Robert; he was in a prickly mood and it would require all her tact. But it had to be done, and soon. Only then could she start rebuilding her life.

CHAPTER NINETEEN

IT WAS noon before Tim was ready to leave for London.

Lindsey was in her bedroom, finishing her packing, when the telephone rang, and without thinking she picked it up. Tim did the same from somewhere else in the house, and as his voice came on the line, so too did Francesca's.

Hearing the lilting Italian accent, Lindsey couldn't resist the temptation to eavesdrop, even though she knew that doing so was nothing short of flagellation.

Francesca, it seemed, was already installed in her home in London.

'The moment I heard on the radio that you had won your bid, I booked my flight back. I'm so happy for you, darling. I can't wait to see you. It seems like years.'

'You were never much good at counting,' he teased.

'I'm very good at other things, don't you agree?'

'How could I not?'

'And I will see you tonight?'

'Yes, you shall.' His voice was unexpectedly serious. 'We have to talk.'

Carefully Lindsey replaced the receiver, her ears ringing with the death knell of all her hopes. Serve her right for being stupid enough to have harboured any! Hadn't she learned anything from Tim's cool behaviour to her these past weeks? Yet she had still believed a miracle could happen.

Well, it hadn't, and she must accept that fact.

Fighting her tears, she closed her cases and went downstairs, tall and elegant in a slate-grey suit that drew the eye to her glowing auburn hair. She might feel like death but she looked the picture of life! Which was precisely the image she wanted Tim to have of her.

'The house will be awfully lonely without you.' Mrs Ramsden, coming into the hall to make her farewell, smiled at her mistily.

'That's what you said every time Tim departed to boarding school,' her husband joked. 'You'll just have to make do with me!'

Lindsey gave her mother-in-law an impetuous hug, and at that moment Tim returned from stowing away the cases. An eyebrow rose at sight of her embracing his mother, and she hastily drew back and went to shake Mr Ramsden's hand. Then picking up the cat basket, she followed Tim to the car.

In a flurry of goodbyes they set off, Lindsey waving until the long driveway curved and the Manor was no longer in sight.

'You and Mother hit it off,' he remarked. 'Both the parents were completely at ease with you.'

'It was the same for me.'

'It never used to be.'

'It never used to be a lot of things, Tim. But times have changed and we've all changed with them.'

He accepted this in silence, and Lindsey leaned back and closed her eyes. But she was painfully aware of the man beside her, her breasts swollen with desire for him, her longing to fling herself into his arms so intense that she trembled with the effort of remaining where she was. If only he had made love to her again! If only she hadn't allowed pride to stop her from trying to seduce him. Yet it wasn't only pride, but the fear of rejection that had kept her restless in her lonely bed, for had she offered herself and been rejected, she might—in her vulnerability—have admitted she loved him.

'We're also giving Jack a lift to London.'

Tim's voice drew her back to the present, and she sat up, glad they weren't going to be alone. 'I thought he had his car here.'

'A van skidded into it last night. Luckily he wasn't in it.'

Case in hand, Jack was waiting in the entrance of the inn, and leapt into the car almost before it stopped. 'I've been waiting half an hour for you.'

'Sorry. I was held up. I meant to let you know but I forgot.'

'That's not like you.'

'I had things on my mind.'

Francesca, Lindsey thought bleakly, and gave him a quick, sidelong glance. Tiredness had robbed his skin of colour, and deepened the fine lines at the corners of his eyes. The urge to hold him close and press his head to her breast, caused her to make an involuntary movement, and he gave her a sharp glance which she met with a blank one.

'I'm planning on buying a house in Evebury.' Tim abruptly changed the topic. 'Much as I enjoy staying with my parents at weekends, I need the privacy of my own home.'

Lindsey knew why, and the blackness of despair settled round her like a shroud. It did not lift until they arrived at Smith Street, after dropping Jack at Sloane Square, and Lindsey felt a sense of homecoming as she entered the house, where the Parkers were waiting to congratulate Tim.

There was a stack of messages on the table, and a case of vintage champagne from Francesca. He immediately opened one of the bottles and poured out four glasses.

'To your continuing success,' Parker said. 'I don't know anyone who deserves it more.'

He and his wife raised their glasses and Lindsey did the same, though she barely swallowed a mouthful. Toasting Tim with Rodier Crystal from his future wife was more than she could stomach!

'Will you both be dining at home?' Mrs Parker enquired as she and her husband left the room.

'We'll let you know later,' Tim promised.

Alone with him, Lindsey set down her glass. 'I won't be here to dinner. I'm moving back to my apartment.'

'You must be keen to pick up the threads of your life?'

'Naturally.' She wished she knew how he'd react if she told him that after tonight she wouldn't be seeing Robert, and that before the week was over she planned to be in New York. Not that she had any intention of telling him. The two men were unlikely to meet, and with luck Tim might never discover that they hadn't married.

'I'll instruct my lawyer to seek a divorce on the grounds of irreconcilable breakdown,' he said into the silence. 'I'd also like to discuss our financial arrangements. If you can arrange for your lawyer to——'

'I don't want anything from you, Tim. I never banked the cheques you sent me, as I'm sure you're aware, and I'm not about to start accepting money from you now.'

'You're my wife and you're entitled to a settlement.'

'I'm not. *I* left *you*, not the other way around.'

'You left because you misjudged the situation between myself and Patsy.'

'I should have had more trust in you.'

He shrugged, the gesture intimating that it was all water under the bridge, and no longer of any import.

'I don't want your money,' she reiterated. 'Now if you'll excuse me, I'd like to get on with my packing.'

She hurried to her room before he could answer, intent on reaching it before she gave way to tears. Yet alone there, the tears did not come, and she was proud of the sudden calmness she felt as she put her cases on the bed and methodically filled them.

The phone rang frequently, though only after several calls did the buzzer on her table sound, and she lifted the receiver to hear Robert on the line.

'I'm free earlier than I thought,' he said without preamble. 'I can come and collect you.'

'I'd rather you didn't.'

'You *are* leaving, aren't you?'

'Very shortly.'

'Good. I'll be with you in an hour. I'm too impatient to wait till this evening.'

Glad that she would be able to clear the air between them sooner rather than later, she completed her packing, telephoned for a cab, and then went in search of Nuisance.

She found him lapping a saucer of milk in the kitchen, Mrs Parker watching him fondly.

'He's grown to twice his size,' the woman said. 'You've been overfeeding him.'

'He overfed himself. He had a field day with the field mice!'

'Well, he won't find any here—I hope!'

Lindsey smiled. 'When he's finished his milk, would you put him in his basket, please, and leave him by the front door?'

'Are you taking him to the vet, then?'

'The vet? Oh, no, he isn't ill. I—I'm leaving here today.' She avoided the housekeeper's eyes. 'Would you ask Parker to bring down my cases?' She held out her hand. 'Thank you for taking care of me while I was here. My husband is very lucky to have you and Parker taking care of him.'

Before the woman could reply Lindsey hurried out, and as she reached the hall she heard the chug of a taxi drawing to a stop outside. Opening the door, she waved to show that she knew he was there, then went into the living-room where Tim was still sorting through his messages.

'I'm leaving now, Tim. I just want to wish you well.'

'Thank you. Same here.'

He followed her out, his fair hair turned to gold by the slanting rays of the afternoon sun that shone through the window on the first floor landing. Almost at once he saw Nuisance in his box.

'I'd forgotten you'd be taking him.' He picked up the cat box and tickled the Siamese's ears. 'I'll miss the little devil.'

She noted he didn't say he'd miss *her*. But then Tim had always disliked lying.

'If I'd realised Lawson wasn't collecting you,' he added, 'I'd have driven you myself.'

He placed the cat box in her arms, falling silent as Parker came down the stairs with her cases and carried them out.

Thinking that someone should be playing the overture to *Pagliacci*, Lindsey went down the steps and climbed into the cab, resolutely staring ahead as they rumbled off. From now on she wasn't going to look back. It was the future that held her salvation.

Walking into the empty apartment, she felt so bereft, so much a stranger here, that she wished it were possible to fly to the States today. But she couldn't leave without saying a personal goodbye to her friends, whose discretion she could rely on, or telephoning Mrs Chapman to explain why she could not accept her offer to work for her.

She had better call Phil Marsham in New York too, and after opening the windows to let in some fresh air, and releasing Nuisance, who at once curled up on his favourite cushion, she did.

Phil's pleasure at hearing she was returning to New York did much to ease her battered spirit, making her realise how wounded she was by Tim's rejection of her.

'Where will you stay?' he asked. 'You sublet your apartment, didn't you?'

'On a monthly basis only. It falls vacant this Friday so I can move in.'

'Great. I can't tell you how delighted I am that you're rejoining us. Have dinner with us on Saturday.'

She agreed, and was still enfolded in his warm affection when the doorbell rang. Heart beating heavily, and hating what she had to do, she opened the door to Robert.

Big and bluff, he was as handsome as ever, his business defeat seemingly making no difference to his confident attitude.

'These past weeks have been hell without you,' he muttered, holding her tightly to his chest.

Lost for words, she tried to extricate herself, but he held on to her as they went into the sitting-room.

'You're lovelier than ever,' he said thickly, touching her hair with a proprietorial gesture. 'You've grown it longer.'

'I didn't fancy the village stylist!'

'I'm glad. I prefer it this way.' He rubbed his cheek against hers, breathing her in deeply. 'Mmm, you don't know how much I've been longing to do this. Have you missed me?'

'I was too busy to miss anyone,' she hedged.

'I'm not anyone. I'm the man you're going to marry.'

Her stomach tightened, and the involuntary movement alerted him that all was not well. Dropping his hands from her, his dark eyes probed her face.

'What's wrong, Lindsey?'

'It won't work,' she blurted out, her intention of leading up to this, exploded by anxiety. 'That's why I wanted time to think it over. Because I wasn't sure. But now I am, and I know I can't marry you.'

Tense and pale, she waited for his anger to explode, but all he did was to move heavily towards the window and lean against the side of it, his back to the light, his face in shadow.

'You're staying with Ramsden, aren't you?' he said impassively. 'I think I always knew it.'

'You're wrong. I'm not going back to him.'

'You don't need to spare my feelings, Lindsey. You can admit the truth.'

'I am. The divorce is going ahead.'

'In that case, why burn your boats?'

'Burn my boats?' she echoed, not understanding what he meant, though perhaps it was truer to say not wishing to understand.

'Why leave me when you've nowhere else to go?' he asked. 'As my wife, you'll have everything you want.'

'I wouldn't marry anyone for material gain, Robert. I don't love you, and I can't live with anyone unless I do. I kept telling you I wasn't sure, but you always ignored it.'

'Maybe you should have worded it more strongly.' His voice roughened. 'I knew I shouldn't have let you go to Ramsden. That's where I made my mistake.'

'You couldn't have stopped me. I make my own decisions.' With an effort she kept control of her temper. 'I wish things could have been different for us. I'm very fond of you, but fondness isn't enough.'

'It *can* be. Take a chance and marry me? Given time——'

'If I don't love you by now, I never will.'

'Maybe you can't love *anyone*—other than Ramsden. I still think you have the hots for him!'

The crudeness of the comment robbed her of any sympathy for Robert, but she still hung on to her temper. Whoever had said there was no fury like that of a woman scorned had forgotten to take men into account!

'Tim is going to marry a lovely Italian girl,' she said evenly, 'and I intend to carry on my career.' She made herself smile. 'Maybe I'm not cut out for marriage. These days, more women are discovering the joy of being able to work without the distraction of a husband and family, and I rather think I'm one of them.'

Uncertainty crossed Robert's face, and his anger ebbed. Being rejected in preference to another man was one thing; being rejected in favour of a career was another—and far more acceptable!

'You may find your work rewarding now, but you might regret it when you're in your forties. That's when you'll start feeling lonely. You're a silly woman, Lindsey, and I'm sorry for you. I'd have made you very happy.'

Not as happy as you'll make me by walking out of my life, she thought silently, and, lowering her head, she kept it there until she heard the front door close behind him.

CHAPTER TWENTY

LINDSEY was treated like the prodigal son when she returned to New York and her old job at the television station. Everything was the same, yet not the same, though she was fully aware that the difference lay with herself.

When she had lived here before, she had never fully accepted that she might make America her permanent base, always hoping that one day she and Tim might get back together. But now she accepted that it was not to be, and knew it was time to set down roots and make this her home.

Phil was more than pleased when she told him this. She had given him and Belle an edited version of what had happened in England, but he was perceptive enough to read between the lines and guess something of her heartbreak, though sensitive enough not to mention it.

As summer gave way to autumn, she began work on her first documentary for the new series. Six were planned, and her days were so busy supervising scripts and organising camera crews for the location work that she could think of nothing else, while her nights slipped by in exhausted sleep.

At the end of November, Tim arrived in Washington with a trade delegation, for a four-day visit that included a meeting with the President. Normally it would have merited a paragraph in the more serious news papers, but because he had the blond good looks of a film star, plus wit and charm to boot, the media went wild over him.

Lindsey could not pick up a newspaper without reading about him, or switch on her TV without hearing his cool, cultured voice, and seeing his fine-boned face with its chiselled nose and well-shaped mouth set in lines of firm control, a control she had once had the power to undo...

Of course seeing him like this was *her* undoing, and when, three days after his arrival, she received a letter from her lawyer informing her that her marriage had been dissolved, she was totally bereft.

I'm free, she told herself, but though she repeated the word over and over it held no meaning for her. How could she be free of Tim when her heart still belonged to him? But that was her secret and no one must know it.

But next day, when she read that he was spending Thursday and Friday in New York—which meant he was probably already here—she became completely unravelled.

'You feeling OK?' her assistant, Maggie, asked when Lindsey had twice asked her the same question.

'I've a lousy headache.'

'You're working too many late nights. We're way ahead of schedule and you can afford to take it easy.'

'Save your breath,' Phil Marsham observed, coming into the room and hearing Maggie's remark. 'Don't you know your boss is a workaholic?'

Shaking her head, Maggie left them, and Phil put a hand on Lindsey's shoulder.

'She's right, you know,' he said seriously. 'You've worked flat out since you came back, but these past few days you've been manic.'

'I'm always the same at the beginning of a series,' Lindsey lied.

'You sure it isn't to do with Timothy Ramsden being over here?'

Lindsey went motionless. Trust Phil to get to the heart of the matter. But she respected him too much to go on lying, and with a sigh she leaned back in her chair and met his compassionate gaze.

'Stupid, aren't I?' she said flatly. 'You'd think I'd have come to terms with the situation by now.'

'It would help if you accepted some of the invitations that come your way, instead of being nursemaid to two cats.'

'I don't disagree with you there. Maybe I'll feel more sociable in the New Year.'

'Your New Year's beginning tonight,' Phil stated, his stocky frame taking on a belligerent stance. 'Belle and I are going to Dick Ferman's party,' he named a well-known author, 'and I know he'd be happy to see you. We'll pick you up at seven-thirty.'

Appreciating the kindness of the suggestion, Lindsey felt obliged to accept it, and at lunchtime decided to buy a new dress and put herself in a party mood.

She went to Barney's, emerging an hour and a half later with a slither of black velvet that, when on, turned her into an auburn-haired siren. Of course she succumbed to a pair of matching shoes, and then espied a dream of a theatre coat in emerald satin which had been created just for her, as had a nifty little suit in French blue.

But why shouldn't she splash out on herself? Her career was firing on all cylinders, and if she accepted a rival TV station's offer to do her own chat show she would be even more successful. To date, she had always given the thumbs-down to such an offer, but she was no longer against it, for it would give her a more socially exciting life. Less cerebral, of course, but that might be an advantage.

Musing on this, she waited at the kerb for a taxi. A dozen careered past her, and she was growing impatient when one finally stopped to let out a passenger.

Signalling it to wait for her, she stepped back as a slender, curvaceous brunette emerged, swathed in cream cashmere, silky black hair cascading over the voluptuously large shawl collar.

Francesca! Who else would a malicious fate have thrown at her?

'Lindsey!' came the lilting voice. 'How lovely to see you again. What are you doing here?'

'Shopping.'

Only as Lindsey heard herself did she realise what a daft answer she had given. Francesca obviously knew from Tim that she was supposed to be marrying Robert, and must be curious to know why she was in New York and not London.

'I had several things to sort out here,' she added hastily. 'And to buy too.' Deliberately she glanced down at the numerous packages she was holding, trying to inject some insouciance into the conversation.

'A trousseau?' Francesca exclaimed, practically clapping her hands. 'I bought mine in Italy, of course, but when I'm here I can't resist Barney's.'

'I suppose you were with Tim in Washington too?' Lindsey said.

'No, I wasn't. I find all those business dinners so boring that I went to stay with friends in Virginia. But tonight he's guest of honour at a party at the Plaza, so I flew in for it. We're returning to London on Sunday!'

'Hey, lady!' a throaty growl interrupted them. 'I ain't got all day to hang around. You hiring me or not?'

'Yes, I am,' Lindsey said, grateful for the interruption, and with a hurried goodbye to Francesca climbed into the cab.

Don't cry, she ordered herself. You've learned nothing new, and nothing has changed. You knew Tim was going to marry her when he was free, and you have to start building a new emotional life for yourself.

With a determination she normally reserved for her career, Lindsey launched herself into the social whirl. The 'little black dress' she had bought the day she had bumped into Francesca turned out to be as successful as she had hoped, and her circle of men-friends grew by leaps and bounds. But unfortunately none of them meant anything to her, and as Christmas approached, and with it more and more invitations to parties, she found it increasingly difficult to cope with the festivities going on around her. And there was still a week to go until Christmas Day and a long weekend of partying!

But how to avoid it?

It wasn't until Belle rang and insisted she spend the holidays with her and Phil at their chalet in Aspen that Lindsey knew what she had to do.

'I'll be in Paris,' she lied. 'I'm spending a week there.'

'Paris? That's very sudden, isn't it?'

'It was a sudden invitation.'

'Aha! Who is he?'

Lindsey hesitated, then took advantage of Belle's romantic streak. 'We—er—we'd like to keep it quiet for the moment.'

'If he's married, don't go.'

'He isn't.'

'Then why can't you tell me who——?'

'Secrecy lends excitement, don't you think?'

'Yes, I do, but I still want to know who he is! Call me the minute you get back.'

The lie Lindsey had uttered on the spur of the moment left her with no option other than actually to go to Paris, and suddenly it didn't seem such a crazy idea. It was a cop-out, she acknowledged that, but why shouldn't she do exactly as she pleased? Indeed, why didn't she please herself one hundred per cent and really live it up?

With this in mind, she didn't book a room in a small hotel on the Left Bank, as she had originally intended, but took one at the Ritz. Lonely she might be in the city of lovers, but at least she'd be lonely in luxury!

Three days before Christmas, outwardly joyful but inwardly wishing she were going to Aspen after all, she left her two cats with her neighbours and departed for the airport.

There were surprisingly few people travelling abroad, and after checking in she browsed in the bookstore, searching for something interesting to occupy her evenings.

She was at the check-out, a pile of books in her arms, when there was a tap on her shoulder, and, swinging round, she saw Jack Dunford, rumpled as always, his small eyes shrewd as ever.

'Hello, Lindsey. This is an unexpected pleasure. How are you keeping?'

'Fine. And you?'

'Couldn't be better. You on your way back?'

'Back?' she echoed.

'To England?'

She nodded, marvelling that within the course of a month she had seen both Francesca and Jack, two people she could well have done without meeting.

'What have *you* been doing here?' she asked, determinedly swinging the conversation his way.

'I was in Washington with Tim, then decided to take a long break and explore the southern states. I arrived in New York a couple of weeks ago.'

Lindsey's scalp prickled. If Jack had been here this length of time, he had probably read some of the rave reviews that had surrounded her last documentary, and would know she was working here again.

'Do you have time for a coffee?' he suggested.

There was no way she could refuse, and she went with him to a nearby cafeteria and sat at a table while he collected two coffees.

'I bumped into Francesca when she was here,' Lindsey said as he settled himself opposite her. As long as she was controlling the conversation she might stand a chance of keeping it away from herself. 'When is the wedding?'

'February. When is yours? Or is your career taking precedence?'

So he *did* know she had returned to the television station. Giving a slight lift of her shoulders, she said casually, 'Why should a career take precedence over marriage? It's possible to combine both if there's give and take on both sides.'

'So who's doing the commuting—you or Lawson?' Jack leaned across the table. 'Or is there a third possibility?'

'A third?'

'That neither of you is commuting? That you aren't seeing Lawson any longer?'

Lindsey moistened lips that had unexpectedly gone dry, annoyed at having underestimated this man's perspicacity. But there was no reason why she couldn't lie her way out of it.

'I have to complete my contract with Universal TV, and until I have the marriage is on hold.'

'Is that why you look so miserable?'

'Thanks.'

'Sorry, but it's true. I was watching you when you were choosing some books, and I thought you looked as bloody miserable as Tim.'

Lindsey couldn't hide her surprise. 'Why should he be miserable?'

'I was hoping *you'd* know the answer to that.' Jack's lower lip jutted forward. 'From the look of you, I'd say you're both suffering from love-sickness!'

Lindsey slapped down her cup on its saucer. 'I don't find your sense of humour funny.'

'I wasn't being humorous. I'm serious.'

Anxiously she glanced at her wristwatch. Anticipating a Christmas rush, she had arrived here far too early, and still had half an hour to wait before her flight was called.

'Look, Jack, I don't know what game you're playing and I'm not interested in Tim enough to care, but if he has problems and you want to talk them over with someone, then the person you should be discussing them with is Francesca.'

'Tim isn't *her* problem.'

'Well, he damn well isn't mine!' Lindsey stopped abruptly. 'What do you mean, he isn't *her* problem?'

'Why should he be? Fact is, she'd be tickled pink to know he's unhappy as hell.'

Lindsey felt like Alice, lost in a strange Wonderland. 'If they're getting married in February why should she be pleased that——?'

'Who said she's marrying him in February?'

'You did. A few moments ago.'

Jack shook his head. 'You misunderstood me. Francesca's getting married in February all right—but not to Tim. The day after you left Smith Street, they broke up.'

Lindsey swallowed hard. 'But I—I overheard him speaking to her on the telephone that same morning. He was going to see her that night and ask her to marry him.'

'You got it wrong,' Jack said bluntly.

'Oh, come on! I might have misconstrued *one* conversation, but there were too many other times when he spoke of her in loving terms.'

'A smokescreen,' Jack declared. 'He loves *you*. He always has.'

'Then why did he let me go without trying to stop me?'

'He thought you loved Robert Lawson. He still does.'

Lindsey leaned back in her chair, her brain whirling with conflicting emotions. Was Jack speaking the truth? Did Tim still love her? Had she misjudged him again?

'Has he actually told you he loves me?' she asked.

'Not in words. But I saw the way he looked at you when you weren't watching him.' Jack's mouth curled mischievously. 'I also saw the way you looked at him! I may be a crusty old bachelor but I can recognise love when I see it. You aren't really going to marry Lawson, are you?'

'No,' she confessed.

'Then call Tim and tell him.'

'Why can't he call me?'

'He would if I recounted this conversation to him. But do you honestly want me to act as go-between? Wouldn't you rather tell him yourself, or is pride stopping you?'

'I loathe that word! It's caused me far too much misery.'

'Then go and see him.'

Lindsey fell silent. If Jack was wrong about Tim's feelings she would end up with egg on her face. But so what! She had wasted too many years to let more time slip by.

'You're right,' she declared. 'I'll see him as soon as——' She stopped. 'I can't! I'm not going to England. I'm booked on a flight to Paris!'

'I see.'

Jack's tone held a wealth of meaning, all of it wrong, and Lindsey shook her head at him. 'I'm not meeting a man there, if that's what you think. I'll be on my own. I couldn't face the jollity here and had to get away from it.'

Jack's face softened and he jumped to his feet. 'Come on! We must hurry!'

'Where are we going?'

'To book you on my flight to London.'

'But what about my luggage? If I don't check in, it will cause a security alert!'

'Hell, I forgot that! I'll ask the British Embassy to sort it out.'

'Why should *they* help me?'

'Because you're the wife of a very prominent man.'

'I was divorced a few weeks ago!'

'It won't be final for another month, so keep your mouth buttoned and watch diplomacy at work!'

Within twenty minutes Lindsey had permission to board Jack's flight to London, and her luggage was allowed to travel to Paris without her accompanying it.

'Pity the Embassy couldn't get my cases transferred,' she commented as they made their way to the aircraft.

'There wasn't time. But the Embassy in Paris will arrange to collect them and hold them for you.' Brown eyes twinkled at her. 'Once you're back with Tim, I guarantee you won't give a damn about your clothes!'

If Jack was right, she definitely wouldn't, Lindsey thought as she sat beside him on the seemingly never-ending journey across the Atlantic. Trouble was, one moment she was convinced she had done the right thing to change her booking, and the next she was equally sure she had made a horrible mistake.

'Tim may be in Evebury,' she murmured as they began their descent to London at six-thirty next morning.

'He's in town working on a speech he has to give early in January. I spoke to him yesterday and he said he won't be going to his parents' until Christmas Eve.' A gentle hand lightly touched her arm. 'If you want to have a rest and then freshen up before you see him, you're welcome to come to my place.'

'Thanks for the offer, but I'll check into a hotel for the day. I'm not sure when I'll go to see him.'

'You won't chicken out, will you?'

'No. But it will take courage.'

'I don't think you're short of that,' Jack said, but she noticed with wry amusement that he insisted on remaining with her until she had booked into the Berkeley Hotel, and then made sure she had his telephone number.

'Don't hang around here too long,' he advised as he left her. 'Imagination can play havoc with your nerves.'

She admitted this four hours later when, bathed and rested, she finally faced the prospect of going to see Tim. Critically she surveyed herself. Used to travelling in her job, she had learned the art of being comfortable without being sloppy and, anticipating arriving at the Paris Ritz, she had chosen a simple shirtwaister in finest cream cashmere, with a matching cashmere coat several shades darker and slightly heavier in weight.

On an impulse she leaned towards the mirror and removed the gold barette that held her silky auburn hair away from her face. Instantly it swung forward, the ends curving softly against the shadowed hollows beneath her cheekbones. Adding a touch of lipstick to her trembling lips, she picked up her purse and went down to settle her bill.

Where would she be tonight? In heaven, in Tim's arms, or alone at the Ritz in Paris, in a luxurious, empty hell?

CHAPTER TWENTY-ONE

THE journey to Chelsea seemed never ending, and as Tim's house came into view Lindsey nearly lost her nerve and asked the driver to head to the airport. But if she did, could she face the torment of a life without him? A soft moan escaped her. No, she couldn't. She would do anything rather than accept such a future.

Stepping from the cab, she hurriedly paid the fare and mounted the steps to the front door. Drawing a deep breath, she pressed the bell.

Hardly had her hand dropped to her side when the door was opened by Parker. His pleasure at the sight of her gave her a warm feeling, but as he went to speak she put her finger to her lips. He understood immediately and inclined his head towards the library.

Not giving herself time to think, she sped across the hall, silently turned the handle and went in.

Tim was at his desk, a document in his hand, but he was not reading it. He was staring into space and wasn't aware of her presence. The anguish on his face was a mirror image of her own and, unwilling to be an intruder on such pain, she announced her presence by sharply closing the door.

The sound jolted him back to the present and he turned towards it. Seeing her, he frowned—as if not trusting what his eyes were showing him—then jumped to his feet.

'Lindsey! What are you doing here? Is anything wrong?'

'No. I—I wanted to see you.'

He came round the side of the desk and, despite the casual looseness of his grey cashmere sweater and darker grey trousers, she noticed how thin he had become. His skin had lost its natural glow and there were shadows beneath his eyes. If their parting had dealt unkindly with her, it had dealt even more unkindly with him, and it was all she could do not to rush forward and gather him into her arms; to hold him close and tell him that no matter what, she would never leave him again.

'Why do you want to see me?' he asked.

At the coldness of his voice her courage deserted her. Had Jack got it wrong? Was it Francesca who had changed her mind about marrying Tim and not the other way around? If so, Jack could well have decided that bringing Lindsey back into Tim's life was the best solution. She went hot with embarrassment, then icy cold with anger at the subtle way the man had manipulated her. Resolutely she set about saving face.

'I—I bumped into Jack and he—he told me Francesca was marrying someone else.'

Nonchalantly Tim leaned against the edge of the desk. 'Don't tell me you've come to commiserate?'

'Hardly.' Lindsey clenched her hands. Tim was not behaving as she had anticipated, and she couldn't, she absolutely couldn't tell him she loved him. 'Did you—did she leave you because of me?'

'If I said no, would it ease your conscience?'

'I—er——'

'Well, it *was* because of you. And if that makes you feel guilty, too damn bad!'

'You've no reason to be angry with *me*,' Lindsey retorted. 'I only went back to you to help you.'

'I know.' The anger left Tim's voice and he half turned away from her. 'I'm sorry. I'm in a lousy mood. I appreciated what you did, and I'm glad for your sake that Lawson was so understanding.'

'I thought Francesca was too. When I saw her——' Lindsey stopped, then said in a rush, 'Would it help if I called and told her she has no reason to be jealous of me?'

There was a long silence, broken only when Tim turned and looked directly into her eyes. 'She wouldn't believe you. You see, I said exactly the opposite when I left her.'

Lindsey stared at him.

'Don't look so stunned,' he chided. 'And for God's sake don't go all guilty on me. I learned to live without you before, and I can do so again.'

'I hope not!' she cried. 'Because I can't live without *you*! Oh, Tim, you idiot! I love you. I always have—I always will!'

For a split-second he was motionless, then with a muttered oath he reached out and pulled her into his arms. He made no attempt to kiss her, just held her close and breathed in the scent of her. She felt the warmth of his body, the tremble of his limbs, and relaxing against him, knew she had finally and irrevocably come home.

'Why didn't you tell me how you felt?' he questioned huskily. 'I thought you were already married to Lawson.'

'I never agreed to marry him. I told him from the beginning that I wasn't sure how I felt about him, but he kept hoping he could make me change my mind. But the minute I saw you again I knew it was hopeless, and I went back to the States.'

'What months we've wasted! I've been demented with jealousy, imagining you as his wife. Why the hell did you let me think you were going to marry him?'

'For the same reason you let me think you were going to marry Francesca!'

'What fools we were.'

'Francesca didn't help,' Lindsey said bluntly. 'When I saw her in New York she——'

'You saw her there?' Tim pulled back a few inches the better to see Lindsey's face.

'Yes. I bumped into her outside Barney's—a dress store. That's when she told me she'd bought her trousseau in Italy and—oh, everything she said was calculated to make me believe she was marrying you in a couple of months.' Lindsey frowned. 'If you'd walked

out on her, how come she was going to the party that
was given for you in New York?'

'That's a good question,' Tim drawled. 'Particularly
as she wasn't invited.'

'She was lying?'

'In her back teeth. But enough of her. It's us I want
to talk about. I should never have let you leave me. I
made a mistake not fighting to keep you five years ago,
and when you came back into my life I made the same
mistake again.' His voice was low, his words running
into each other as if he wished to get them quickly said.
'But I loved you then and I love you now—more if that's
possible.'

'You did a great job hiding it,' Lindsey chided. 'Didn't
you have any inkling how I felt when I came back to
you during the takeover bid?'

'I assumed it was a sense of duty.'

'And when I went to bed with you—was that also out
of duty?'

'I put it down to chemistry,' he confessed wryly. 'And
you were so cool and uncaring next morning that I followed your lead and acted the same way.'

'If you knew the effort it cost me to pretend...' Lindsey
drew a shuddering breath. 'I was determined not to give
myself away because I thought you were just using me—
that I was the nearest body available.'

'How could you think such a thing? Making love to
you was a sacrament. It always was; it always will be.'

Moved to tears, Lindsey pressed closer to him. 'That's
the nicest thing you've ever said to me. Oh, darling,
forgive me for the way I behaved. I was so wrong not
to believe you when you said you hadn't been to bed
with Patsy, and then I made things worse by taking that
job in America. When I think of the misery I put you
though, I could cut my throat!'

'Messy and unnecessary,' Tim stated firmly. 'The first
year was tough for me, I'll grant you that, but then my
career took off and I put my emotions on hold.'

'Until you met Francesca,' Lindsey couldn't help saying. 'Would you have married her if we hadn't met again?'

'Probably,' he said with honesty. 'She was lightweight and decorative and made no demands on me.'

'The perfect wife!'

'Many men would think so,' Tim grinned. 'But I happen to be stuck on an intelligent and beautiful redhead who quite rightly wants her marriage to be a partnership.' For the first time a shadow of doubt darkened his face. 'My job's a demanding one, darling, and there'll be many times when I'll have to go abroad and leave you.'

'That applies to me too,' Lindsey reminded him. 'You used to get annoyed about it before and——'

'Not so much annoyed with you as angry with myself. I wasn't happy working on a newspaper and I imagined your career taking off and you leaving me behind. I gave you a hard time and I was wrong. So no more talk about my forgiving *you*. You also have to forgive me.'

'Done,' she answered promptly and, twining her arms round his neck, pulled his face down to hers.

His hands moved down her spine to cup her buttocks and press her closer to his thighs. She felt his arousal and desire spasmed through her, weakening her legs and making her clutch at him. With a groan he began kissing her, soft, tender kisses on her eyelids, the tip of her nose, the side of her cheek before finally reaching her mouth. As their lips met, hers parted, and his tongue, moist and hot, drove deeply into her.

Passion mounted, and the gentleness of Tim's touch turned to a frenzy of searching that awakened such an intensity of desire that Lindsey felt as if she were drowning in sensual ecstasy.

'I want you,' she gasped. 'I need you...'

'Not here,' he groaned, pushing her away, yet still holding her. 'I don't want to take you on the carpet!'

'Why not? It sounds good to me!'

They smiled at each other, humour easing their need, and Tim reached for the telephone.

'Who are you calling?' Lindsey asked.

'My lawyer, to tell him not to finalise our divorce, and then my parents. I was going to spend Christmas with them, but I'd prefer to stay here alone with you. We've so many things to say to each other I don't want to share you with anyone. We can spend the New Year with them instead.'

'That's exactly how I feel,' Lindsey agreed huskily, moving close to him again as he made the two calls.

'There's one thing I forgot to mention,' Tim murmured as he replaced the receiver. 'The Parkers are going to stay with their daughter for a few days, so we'll have to go out for meals.'

Lindsey laughed. 'How do you feel about pigging it at the Ritz in Paris?'

'Are you serious?'

'Perfectly. That's where I'd be now if I hadn't bumped into Jack at Kennedy Airport. In fact my luggage is already in Paris. It was too late to get it off the plane.'

'Well, that's a perfect reason for us to go there. A lady can't be separated from her luggage, though I guarantee you won't be needing your nightgowns!'

Their eyes met and passion flared, so that when Tim spoke again his voice was thick. 'Keep your distance, sweetheart. If I start kissing you again I won't want to let you go, and I must book our flights and pack my case.'

'I'll see to the flights,' she promised.

'Good. If there's any problem I'll charter a plane.'

'Such extravagance!'

'To have you to myself I'd willingly charter a rocket!'

Her eyes sparkled and he took a step towards her, stopped with a shake of his head, and then strode out.

By the time he returned, their flights were booked and Parker was waiting outside in the car.

'Everything all right?' Tim asked her.

Lindsey watched him as he came towards her. He seemed a different man from the one she had seen half an hour earlier. There was a glow about him, reflected in the gold of his hair and the faint flush that stained his high cheekbones. How patrician and controlled he was. Yet not so controlled if one looked at him closely, for his bottom lip moved sensuously as he drew nearer, and little flames sparked in his eyes, hinting at passion banked.

'Any problems?' Tim reiterated as she went on staring at him.

'None. Things couldn't be better.'

Reaching for her hand, he drew her out of the room. 'Yes, they can, my darling. Much, much better—as you'll soon find out.'

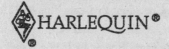

HARLEQUIN®

PRESENTS Plus

"Virgin or wanton?" Oliver Lee is suspicious of everything and everyone.... When he meets Fliss, he thinks her innocence is an act. Fliss *may* be innocent, but the passion Oliver inspires in her is just like raw silk—beautiful, unique and desirable. But like raw silk it is fragile....Only love will help it survive.

Ben Claremont seemed to be the only man in the world who didn't lust after Honey's body...but he asked her to marry him anyway! Honey wasn't in love with him—so separate rooms would suit her just fine! But what on earth had she gotten herself into? Were their wedding vows based on a lie?

Presents Plus—the Power of Passion!

Coming next month:

Raw Silk by Anne Mather
Harlequin Presents Plus #1731

and

Separate Rooms by Diana Hamilton
Harlequin Presents Plus #1732

Harlequin Presents Plus
The best has just gotten better!

Available in April wherever Harlequin books are sold.